BAD RIVER

S.J. King

CHEYENNE CROSSING PRESS

Copyright © 2012, S.J. King

All rights reserved. No part of this book may be reproduced, scanned, or distributed in any printed or electric form without permission. Please do not participate in or encourage piracy of copyrighted materials in violation of the author's rights. Purchase only authorized editions.

Library of Congress Cataloging-in-Publication data

King, S.J.

Bad River/S.J. King

1. Kerlan, Sam (Fictitious character)---Fiction 2. Drummond, Hiram (Fictitious character)---Fiction I. Title

This is a work of fiction. Names, characters, places, and incidents either are the product of the author's imagination or are used fictitiously, and any resemblance to actual persons, living or dead, businesses, companies, events or locales is entirely coincidental.

Cover art from the painting 'Deadwood Freight" by South Dakota Artist Mick Harrison (background of painting from archival photo of pioneer Deadwood)

"BAD RIVER"

S.J. King has generously offered to provide the Avera St. Luke's Gift Shop with donated copies of his new book and 100% of the proceeds will go to fund a special project of the Avera St. Luke's Auxiliary. This project will provide digital thermometers to every baby born here at St. Luke's Birthplace throughout the year.

Your purchase of one book contributes to this project providing three thermometers for three newborns and their family and potentially saving lives!

BAD RIVER

For my Father:

Had he lived in an earlier time he would have opened ranges, pushed the frontier westward, and stood up to the bad elements

And, for Pete Long:
A real cowboy, and friend

Chapter One

The gloom of the office stood in stark contrast to the brightness of the clear autumn day. The dark mahogany wood, cigar stained tin-type ceiling, and masculine austerity suited the man's view of the world. The occupant of this sanctum sanctorum was a man who had spent a life in the careful anticipation of events, fluctuations of markets, and vicissitudes of commerce. He had been cautious, circumspect, and strategic in his machinations. He was alone, but stoically content within that loneliness.

Hiram Drummond pored over his accounts. Since Mrs. Drummond passed away the year before he found himself immersed again in the day-to-day affairs of his bank and mining company. The claims were paying fairly well with the exception of the Liz Anne on Grizzly Bear Creek. He suspected that the Canady brothers were putting some of that wash gold down their boots, but he wasn't going to accuse anyone, for the claims weren't producing what they were in the mid-seventies. The day before he had sent out his overseer, Jack Catlin, and he would hopefully receive a proper accounting later in the morning.

Drummond wandered into the Black Hills during the early days of the rush. He picked up work in a Deadwood saloon keeping the books for Billy Donovan. Donovan was a boisterous Irishman who never possessed good business sense. In time, he became envious of the fortunes being made by the new arrivals in the Hills and staked his own claim. To find the grubstake he sold his saloon to Drummond. Many in Deadwood assumed that Drummond had cheated Donovan out of the business, but in truth it had only been Drummond's astute accounting skills that had kept Donovan's operation afloat. Donovan's idea of profit reinvestment more than often entailed taking another bottle of Irish whiskey down from the larder and sharing it around among his cronies.

From this humble beginning Drummond built a small empire. He opened a general merchandizing store to sell supplies and equipment, and set up a bank to grubstake miners and their claims. Always ready to foreclose at the first opportunity, Hiram Drummond wasn't well liked in Deadwood. He was, however, respected; the kind of respect men garner to themselves through wealth and power.

Drummond was a man of few friends; one of the select had been Bill Hickok. They would often sit together at the Number Ten Saloon and play cards. Whenever there was trouble in town or out in the gold fields, Hickok was the one man Drummond could rely on for help. It was Hickok who had introduced him to his future wife, Elizabeth Anne O'Daly, a singer and dancer who had come to town to play the lead in a Gilbert and Sullivan musical. So, it was doubly devastating when Drummond heard that Jack McCall had gunned down his friend at the Number Ten Saloon.

Everyone in Deadwood recognized that Elizabeth Anne Drummond was a lady. She had the bearing of royalty, but could still charm the man in the street. She was a favorite of the people of Deadwood, and for them she even took the edge off her husband's questionable business dealings. It was said that Drummond became a more honest man after he married Elizabeth Anne. He began to donate to charity and was known on occasion to give a second, or even third, chance to debtors, particularly if Mrs. Drummond took an interest and put in a good word. The Drummonds would host a party for the town's children each Christmas in their Victorian mansion above Deadwood.

This Irish showgirl turned town Matriarch was the joy of Hiram Drummond's life. When she took to bed and died of consumption he mourned forlornly for months. In his grief he returned to the routine of his bachelor days, sinking himself in the daily drudgery of business affairs in order to escape the painful memories.

Drummond opened his safe and placed in it the accounts of the past week. Hearing some commotion in the street, he shut the safe door. He pulled on his Prince Albert coat and fixed his hat firmly on his head. As he stepped out of his office he glanced up the street to see Jack Catlin coming toward him on horseback, tethering another horse behind him on which was draped a large, tarp covered bundle. Drummond thought Catlin had brought back some equipment in need of repair, or had shot a deer while riding back from the Liz Anne.

"I don't pay you to hunt for yourself, Catlin," Drummond said as the horses rode up to him.

"Wasn't doing any hunting, Mr. Drummond," Catlin said as he dismounted his horse, "but seems like somebody else was." As he spoke, he walked over to the packhorse and pulled off the tarp. Stretched over the back of the animal were the lifeless bodies of the Canady brothers.

"Damn, they've done it again," Drummond said in disgust, and with anger in his voice. "I thought I'd seen the end of this."

"The boys' were dead a day or so afore I found them. The gold they washed from the stream was gone along with their boots, guns and stores. Same as what happened to Potts and Culver over at Potato Creek."

Drummond had regained his composure. "Take them over to the furniture store. Tell them pine will do. They have no kin so have Preacher Walker bury them in the morning. After you're through, come back to the office."

Drummond watched as Catlin led the horses up the street. He knew this was yet another challenge to what he had built in the Black Hills. When two of his men had been killed last month at Potato Creek, he felt it might have been an isolated incident. Now he could see a pattern developing. In the early days of the rush there had been a lot of claim jumping. When the gold started to thin out the bad elements had moved on to greener pastures. Hearst had brought in the Pinkertons, and Drummond had a few hired guns himself. Things had settled down until a few months ago when word reached town that Gil Stuart had led a gang into the Hills, and was robbing and murdering settlers and miners. Drummond had the most to lose from Stuart's activity. He had several working mines and washes in the Hills, and was still taking out a sizable amount of gold. He realized that he alone was in a position to confront the Stuart gang.

Drummond was sitting at his desk, drawing heavily on a cigar, when Catlin came back to the office.

"Everything's been attended to, Mr. Drummond. The funeral will be at sunrise tomorrow. Preacher Walker said he'd work up a fine and suitable talking over the graves."

"He needn't bother," Drummond replied, barely paying attention to what Catlin had said. Catlin stood uneasily for a few moments until Drummond finally spoke.

"It was Gil Stuart."

"Had all the fixin's of such," Catlin answered. "Same as Potts and Bob Culver over at Potato Creek."

"I've got to put a stop to this," Drummond declared. "As far as you know, are there any guns in town?"

"Well, Sir, Ted Wills left town a couple of weeks ago. He was getting a little unsteady anyways, hitting the bottle and such."

"Anyone else?"

"Yeah, yeah, there is someone," Catlin came back slowly. "A man by the name of Kerlan. Sam Kerlan, I believe. Worked over in Wyoming in the Big Horn area for a cattlemen's association, cutting fence and the like until he got fed up with it. A'fore that he did a little bounty work down in New Mexico Territory. Don't know much else about him, 'cept he seems like a man who knows what to do with a gun."

"Where did you hear all this?" Drummond demanded.

"From a stage driver."

"Why is he in town?" Drummond inquired again.

"Just passin' through, seems."

Drummond thought for a moment, pulling on his greying beard. "Have this Mr. Kerlan join me for breakfast at Sadie's around eight tomorrow morning. Tell him it could be worth a fair amount of money to him, but tell him nothing more."

"Kerlan," Drummond said softly to himself once Catlin was out of the building. He hadn't heard the name before. This stranger was now his only hope in dealing with Gil Stuart and his murderous gang.

***

A harsh north wind blew over the hillside above Deadwood. As the coffins of the Canady brothers were lowered into the ground, Drummond was thinking of other concerns. Drummond had buried countless bodies, men who had been killed in mine accidents, murdered by roaming Sioux bands or, like the Canady boys, killed by outlaws.

Preacher Walker was halfway through his drawn out eulogy over the graves. Drummond considered Walker the typical sky pilot, uneducated to the point of oblivion, yet pompous in an irritating fashion. "What an ass," Drummond said softly to himself as he waited for the ceremony to end. As Walker continued his seemingly endless sermon, Drummond caught Catlin's eye and motioned to him. Catlin sidled over and stood next to his boss.

"Did you get hold of Kerlan?" Drummond demanded softly.

"Yes sir," answered Catlin. "He said he'd meet you at Sadie's."

"Good. I hope we can get some satisfaction from this Mr. Kerlan."

"…as was said so ably in Job, He setteth an end to darkness, and the shadow of death…"

Drummond stared hard for a time at the preacher and stopped him in mid-speech with an abrupt gesture. After swallowing hard, Preacher Walker said, "Well, Lord, we give up to the soil the earthly remains of these young men, remembering Your promise of resurrection and glory to come. Amen."

Drummond turned quickly and walked down the path to the cemetery gate. He paused for a moment at the grave of his old friend Hickok, and tipped his hat in salute. After mounting his horse, he rode slowly down Mount Moriah and back into Deadwood.

***

Sadie's was not the fanciest eatery in Deadwood, but the food was widely known to be the best in town. Sadie had much the same story as many of the business people in Deadwood. She and her husband had come up north from Ogallala, Nebraska to try their luck in the gold fields. When he died in a mining accident, she sold the claim and settled in Deadwood where she cooked meals for some of the larger outfits, later opening her own place on the main street.

Sam Kerlan had been sitting at Sadie's since it opened, carefully nursing his large cup of coffee. He sat at the rear of the café with his back to the wall, a practice learned from years in his line of work. It had been some time since he felt at ease out in public.

He accepted the offer of a refill from Sadie as Drummond and Catlin came through the door. On seeing Kerlan, Drummond nodded and walked slowly to his table.

"Mr. Kerlan, I believe," he said in a formal manner. "My name is Hiram Drummond, and I believe you and I can do a little business together."

Drummond and Catlin sat down, all three waited in silence while Sadie poured more coffee.

Drummond began, "I am a businessman. I am in mining and banking, and have a few other interests around town. When my businesses run smoothly, I am a content man. When something gets in the way of that smooth operation, I remove it. Something has gotten in the way, and I hear from Mr. Catlin that you may be the man to remove it for me."

Catlin shifted in his chair, but Drummond and Kerlan sat perfectly still. Kerlan took a long drink from his coffee cup and said, "I've sort of retired from that line of trade. It would have to be terrible worth my while to start up again."

"I'll make it worth your while." A sum was mentioned, startlingly large for the job.

Catlin sat up. He had never heard his boss offer so much money for a gun in the past. After a stern glance from Drummond, however, he slid back down in his chair.

"That's a generous offer Mr. Drummond," said Kerlan, "but like I said I've been out of the business for some time and I'm not feeling the desire to start up again."

Drummond shot back with a larger sum, hardly waiting for Kerlan to finish speaking. Stuart's threat to his empire was looming. This was no time to hold back, even if it meant surrendering a small fortune.

Kerlan pulled a small cheroot from his waistcoat, lit it, and slowly breathed in the tobacco smoke. He turned his head and looked directly at Drummond for the first time.

"Mr. Drummond," he said deliberately. "I believe you have yourself a deal. I don't want the details now as I have other business today. I'll stop by your office tomorrow morning and we'll talk. Right now, gentlemen, I want to finish my coffee and enjoy my cigar, so I'll say good day to you."

Drummond showed no reaction, although a look of amazement at Kerlan's boldness was all too apparent on Catlin's face. Drummond simply tipped his hat to Kerlan and strode out of the room with Catlin on his heels.

Cigar smoke swirled in the air above him as Kerlan leaned back hard into his chair. Was he ready to face it again? He had wanted to get out of that kind of life, but the offer was too tempting. "One more time," he said to himself. "One more time."

Chapter Two

Sam Kerlan walked out of Sadie's and onto the streets of Deadwood. The autumn air bit crisply, and he turned up his collar against the wind. He stared down the narrow street and watched as the people of Deadwood went about their daily tasks. He envied their simple, steady lives. He felt himself yearning to be free of the violence and bloodshed by which he had been earning his living for so long.

He walked the short distance from Sadie's to the livery stable, and told the man to saddle his horse. He stood at the front of the stable and took the last few draughts from his cigar before crushing it in the dirt.

The stable hand brought the roan out to the street. It was a beautiful, strong, well-cared for animal, and its stance indicated careful breeding. It had been a gift from Esteban Barela, the New Mexican Hacendado, whose ranch stretched over a wide expanse of northern New Mexican Territory. Barela had been grateful for Kerlan's services and had given him the horse along with a silver encrusted saddle and bridle. Kerlan sold the tack, but he had kept the roan.

Kerlan checked the cinch and bridle before mounting his horse, which stood perfectly still. Secure in the saddle, Kerlan turned the reins and rode slowly out of Deadwood.

He knew where he had to go. Kate had written him in Wyoming and told him exactly where she would be. Though he had never been in the area before, Kerlan went forward with confidence.

He had met Kate in Santa Fe. She was an officer's daughter, secure in her station until her father was killed in a shooting over a bad debt. Kate took to working in a local cabana off the plaza, and it was there Kerlan met her. He took her away from that life, and found a place for her to stay outside Taos. They made that little adobe a home while he worked for Senor Barela.

Senor Barela's gun work kept him away for weeks at a time. Kate patiently bore these absences at first, but at last reached her limit. When Kerlan returned after a particularly bad shoot-out near Chama, Kate informed him that she was marrying another man and was moving to the Dakota gold fields where her intended's brother had staked a claim. Kerlan made no response, simply turning away and mounting his horse. He rode slowly away from the adobe he had called home, never to return.

It had been a surprise when last month Kerlan had received a letter from Kate, dated months previously, which told a story that moved even him. Kate's husband had taken a job in a mine. Within a month, he had lost both his legs in an accident. Kate's letter told of how Tom had taken to drink and how he now lay day after day on his bunk in their small cabin, cursing both her and the world. She had begun to take in laundry to support herself and Tom, but now was at her wit's end, feeling drawn between her desire for freedom and duty to her husband.

Kerlan read the letter and knew at once what he must do. He left his work with the cattlemen's association and turned his roan toward the goldfields of Dakota Territory.

They were called Paha Sapa by the Sioux, who considered them sacred. They were beautiful at this time of year, with aspen leaves turning a bright yellow, standing out against the pines like golden coins in the grass.

Kerlan had traveled to the Hills only once before, on a manhunt out of Wyoming Territory. A young wrangler had killed his foreman in Cheyenne over the attentions of a whore, and Kerlan's cattlemen's association sent him out to bring the young man to justice. Kerlan led a small party out of Cheyenne, which followed the wrangler into the Hills. Soon his men gave up the hunt and returned home, but Kerlan persevered and eventually captured the man in the Southern Hills.

He brought the young wrangler back alive to Cheyenne where he was summarily tried and hung. Kerlan never knew if the youth was guilty or not. He seldom made those judgments, leaving them to other men.

The trip out of Deadwood was shorter than he had anticipated, and he soon came to the road he knew would lead to Kate's cabin. He paused to gather his thoughts before coaxing his horse down the pine trimmed path.

Kate was hanging out laundry on a rope between two trees in front of a run down shack. As Kerlan came into the yard, she reacted immediately, exclaiming in a tearful voice, "Sam!"

Kerlan jumped off his horse and stood as she ran to him. They embraced and Sam could not remember Kate ever having held him so tightly.

"Sam, Sam, what have I come to?" she sobbed.

"Now, now Katie," Kerlan uttered softly as he held her close. They broke off their embrace and held hands as they walked down to the creek. After a few moments Kate's quiet and sad voice broke the silence.

"It was wonderful at the beginning," she started. "Tom and I were hopeful about our future in the Hills. He was never half the man you were, Sam, but he was there for me. You have to understand, Sam, I needed someone to stay with me all the time. You were always away, and I was lonesome for someone to be with. When we got to Deadwood, we found that Tom's brother had cheated us and left the Hills with our money. Tom got a job, but became bitter and took to drink. I'm sure this is why he had his accident. That's what Mr. Drummond said." Kerlan was not all that surprised at the mention of Drummond's name.

"I've tried to make the best of it," Kate continued, "but Tom just drinks more and curses more. I don't think I can stand it much longer." Kate again began to cry.

"You don't have to stand it much longer, Katie," Kerlan said, controlling his voice with some effort. "I've got a plan. Trust me completely and I'll set you free from all of this."

"But what of Tom, what of my commitment to him? I can't just walk away and leave him. He's my husband."

"Tom's no good to anyone right now," said Kerlan soothingly. "He's living in his own private hell, and all he wants to do is make you live it with him. I've arranged a divorce for you with a lawyer friend in Cheyenne. It's all legal and above board. I also got a job for you with my friend Senor Barela in New Mexico. He owes me, and he promises to take care of you."

"What about Tom?" Kate questioned helplessly.

Kerlan had to do some quick considering. He had originally planned to shoot the man and put him out of his misery, but Kate's obvious continued concern for him shook Kerlan's resolve. Recalling Kate's mentioning of Drummond's name, it was suddenly clear in Kerlan's mind.

Although Kerlan was a straightforward man, he would tell a bold face lie to St. Pete for a friend, and especially for Kate.

"Drummond," Sam went on, "has a fund set up for his people who hurt themselves working for him. It's a plan he just came up with, or he would have told you about it before now. It ain't much, but it will keep Tom in hardtack and bacon, and a bottle of hooch now and then."

Kate wept quietly to herself and said softly, "The cup has been taken away; the cup has been taken away...."

Though Kerlan did not catch the biblical reference, he plainly understood Kate's relief.

"Yes, Katie, it's gone, it's gone."

***

A white fog swirled through the pine covered hills above Deadwood. The air was cool, and the soft breathing of the few horses along the main street made it seem as if smoke signals were being offered up from camp to camp.

Sam Kerlan took an early breakfast of eggs and a rash of bacon at Sadie's. He sat back for a few quiet moments, and drank the thick, black coffee Sadie dispensed to her customers. Kerlan was thinking of the days ahead. He knew what was being asked of him, as it had been asked of him many times before. He was going out to kill men. Men he never set eyes on before; men who had done nothing to him personally. He would bring them in alive, of course, if they would let him. They seldom did.

He took his last gulp of the strong brew, threw down four coins and strode out onto the street. He put a cheroot between his teeth, lit it, and breathed in the heavy gray smoke, relaxing for a moment in the chill morning air. After several draughts from the cigar, he threw it to the ground and crossed the street to Drummond's office.

He paused for a moment and surveyed the city of Deadwood, musing about how countless dreams had been won and lost in this sleepy little backwater. "Mostly lost," thought Kerlan. He breathed deeply and walked inside the building.

Drummond was sitting at his large roll-top desk, perusing some papers. He didn't look up when Kerlan entered the room, saying in a loud, disinterested voice, "Yes, what is it?"

"I believe we have some business to commence, Mr. Drummond," Kerlan said in an equally noncommittal tone.

Drummond looked up quickly. He rose from his chair. "Yes. I hadn't realized it was this late already. I'm afraid I get a little caught up in my books. Sit here and we'll discuss the arrangements."

Drummond motioned Kerlan over to the large leather chair next to his desk. He waited until Kerlan sat down, rummaged through his desk, and pulled out from under piles of paper a large, cedar cigar box.

"Please, have one. I have them sent up monthly from Denver. The very best. Cuban."

As Kerlan chose and readied his cigar for lighting, Drummond sat back and scrutinized his newly acquired champion. He saw a young man who had an old man's way about him...a young man who had seen much in his brief years.

Cigar smoke began to fill up the oak paneled office as both men drew heavily on their cigars. It was a man's place: burnished oak and brass spittoon, smelling of worn leather and tobacco smoke.

In a relaxed manner Drummond leaned forward in his chair. He took another long draught from his cigar and resumed the conversation.

"How do you like it around Deadwood?" Drummond asked.

Kerlan breathed out cigar smoke and answered, "I don't rightly have an opinion one way or the other. I guess I feel a little closed in...sort of used to the high plains."

"Have you been to the Hills before?" asked Drummond.

"The Southern Hills, down by French Creek. This is my first time up Deadwood way."

"What are your plans?" Drummond asked, more and more curious about this diffident gunman.

"No real plans," Kerlan replied coolly.

Drummond realized that further questioning would be useless. It was time to get down to business.

"When you deal with Stuart's gang, do you intend to take any men with you?"

"I would if there were some good men available. From what I've seen about town, I'll be traveling alone," Kerlan replied.

"You're welcome to take Catlin. He comes across a little slow, but he's a good tracker and a hell of a rifle shot. Uses a Sharps Carbine," Drummond said.

"I just might consider that," responded Kerlan. "And about supplies?"

"You can take anything you need out of my store," Drummond quickly replied, "and if you need more horses and tack, you can charge it to me at the livery. When do you plan to leave?"

"Tomorrow, after the west bound stage leaves town," Kerlan answered. "Which brings me to a favor I have to ask you?"

"Anything, anything at all," Drummond insisted.

Chapter Three

The guns were laid out in a neat row on the bed. Two Colt pistols lay beside a .44 Henry rifle and a trimmed down scattergun. Kerlan had cleaned and oiled them meticulously, and was now going over a list of ammunition and supplies for the journey.

He heard heavy steps coming up the hallway of the wood frame hotel. He knew it could not be someone stalking him, for the person's manner was much too abrupt. The unknown visitor stood for a moment outside the door and then knocked softly.

"Who is it?" Kerlan demanded in an assured voice.

"It's me, Catlin. Mr. Drummond sent me over for your list of supplies."

Kerlan opened the door and nodded for Catlin to enter.

"Mr. Drummond said for me to get anything you need for your trip," Catlin began. "He also said that I was to come with you if'n you were to have me along."

"I thought it over and decided that you just might be needed," Kerlan responded. "I want to assure you that I will be doing the rough work myself and that you will just be along to cover the drags."

Catlin, though not overjoyed at his inclusion, accepted the task before him. He was always ready to do whatever Mr. Drummond asked of him.

"I've written down a few things we're going to need," Kerlan said as he resumed the conversation. "You'll need a good riding horse and a pack horse. I plan to travel light and quiet. When trouble comes I may need you to place a few good rifle shots, but from enough distance that you shouldn't have to worry about your personal safety. But things do go wrong in these situations, and you have to be ready to face whatever comes."

"I've done a little of the work myself," answered Catlin, "and though I don't look for it, I won't run from trouble."

Kerlan looked this strange, lanky hillbilly over and decided that he would do just fine.

"What time does the Cheyenne bound stage leave town?" questioned Kerlan.

"Seven in the morning," Catlin returned.

Kerlan walked over to the bedpost where his coat was hanging. From the inside pocket he removed an envelope and handed it to Catlin.

"There's a legless miner and his wife living down the mountain a bit. He was hurt in an accident and she does laundry. Know them?"

"Yea, I've been by there," Catlin replied, wondering about Kerlan's connection to them.

"After you get the supplies I want you to run this note over to the wife. Give it to the wife and to no one else. Understand?"

Kerlan spoke this last command with such authority that Catlin could only nod vigorously.

"Good. I guess I'll be seeing you in the morning," Kerlan said in a more friendly tone as he opened the door for Catlin to leave.

"The morning, yes sir," Catlin said as he nervously made his way out of the room.

***

The crack in the ceiling reminded him of the Pecos River, a familiar sight during his days working for Barela. He was thinking of New Mexico Territory and Santa Fe, that dusty, little Spanish village below the Sangre de Cristo Mountains. It was a beautiful place, and the memory of its warmth contrasted sharply with the present reality of the Dakota Hills steadying themselves for fall and winter's blast.

He was lying on the bed, conflicting thoughts swirling through his head. He was angry with himself for accepting Drummond's offer, and yet undeniably drawn by the challenge. He wondered if he would ever be able to leave this brutal way of life and start down a new, more peaceful road.

He rose uneasily from the bed and walked over to the window. People were moving up and down the main street; he could hear laughter from the saloons and an occasional horse whinny. He decided he must get out for some air lest his thoughts torment him further.

As he dressed, his mind returned to Kate. Catlin would have delivered the note hours ago, and he pictured Kate both worried and elated. She would be free of her suffocating life, free to begin again. Senor Barela, the Patron of Northern New Mexico, was a powerful and fearless man, but he would be gentle with Kate. Not from any altruistic motives, but in the hope that his kindness to Kate would bring Kerlan's gun back to his service.

He walked out the front door of the hotel and looked down the street, dark but for sprays of light coming from windows and doorways. The night sky was blue and black and starless. The little town seemed powerless against the hulking mountains. The night air was cool. Kerlan shivered, not so much from the cold as from the loneliness of Deadwood without light.

He moved up the street and stopped at a run down shack. Peering in he saw several Chinamen standing by a large plank stretched between two barrels, while others sat sleepily on the floor. The whole scene seemed like a photograph, as the men were completely motionless.

Kerlan continued up the street and stopped outside the Number Ten Saloon. He could hear talking, the occasional burst of laughter, and the muffled sound of a piano. He entered the swinging doors and surveyed the room. There was a long bar to one side over which hung a picture of a naked lady with cupids dancing about her. On the other wall was a lone picture of an English hunt scene with a bullet hole where the lead rider's head should have been.

The bar was not crowded. Several men played cards at a table at the back. Others leaned against the bar, drinking quietly. A piano player plunked heavily on old keys, a tune Kerlan had heard a thousand times before. It seemed he wasn't a total stranger in the saloon, as he noticed Drummond and Catlin sitting over drinks at a small table against the far wall. He nodded and Drummond raised his glass to him. He was in no mood for conversation, and Drummond didn't press him to join his table.

Kerlan asked for a bottle of rye whiskey and poured himself a healthy share in a large tumbler. He sipped the rye and washed it around his mouth before letting it slip down his throat. He took another sip, and leaned into the bar to take the weight off his feet. Surveying the line of men next to him, Kerlan was reminded of horses at a trough.

There was some commotion at the end of the bar. Two miners were arguing, one seemingly trying to quiet the other. The one making the most noise was a chubby, bearded little man who wouldn't have had the courage to say slapjacks without a little who-hit-John in his gut. The other man was tall and thin and had the appearance of someone who wanted to go through life not bothering anyone, on the hope that no one would bother him. Whatever control he had over the fat man was lost as the bearded fellow broke away to the center of the room, where he stood before Drummond and Catlin.

"You cheated us, Drummond," he said in a drunken slur. "We want our money back."

Drummond was apparently accustomed to such encounters, and didn't reply with any haste. He looked up slowly and said in a friendly manner, "Now Mr. Coates, you borrowed that money fair and square. I even gave you extra time. You can ask your partner there. I even let you keep some travel money, which you apparently drank up tonight."

"I want it all, Drummond, or you'll not see another sunrise on this earth," cried the fat man.

With those words Coates drew a Navy Colt from inside his worn jacket. His hand shaking, he pointed the pistol at Drummond. Kerlan was watching the action over his left shoulder and could see that Catlin's Sharps Carbine was leaning against the wall, out of reach. Kerlan pulled his coat away and exposed his pistol, removing the hammer guard in the same smooth motion.

Coates had not yet pulled the hammer back on the Navy. Kerlan waited in the hope that Drummond could calm this drunken miner with his golden tongue.

"Now my good man, see here, I don't want you to leave Deadwood with empty pockets. I'll give you and your friend enough money for the stage out and a little for a new start somewhere. Put that pistol down now and I'll get you a bottle from the bartender."

"I want all the money you owe me now or I'll send you to Hades," answered Coates with a confidence fueled by liquor.

With those words Coates began to draw back the hammer on the Navy. Before it was halfway cocked, Kerlan removed his pistol from its holster, leveled, and fired a round that in the small room sounded like a cannon discharging. The bullet ripped through Coates' wrist, severing his hand. Blood gushed from the wrist and splattered on the floor like water over a falls. Coates screamed in terror and clutched his butchered arm against his chest. He turned a half circle and fell flat on his backside, like a child who had just been knocked to the floor by a bully.

The scene was startling in its quickness. Kerlan, with an almost indifferent calmness, walked forward and directed Catlin to take the wounded man to the local sawbones. Catlin and Coates' partner helped Coates stagger to his feet and out of the saloon.

Drummond sat in wonderment, staring across the room at Kerlan the Shootist as the men took Coates away. Kerlan turned and looked at Drummond. No words were exchanged between the two men. Kerlan returned to the bar and his bottle of rye, while Drummond looked down at the floor where a Navy Colt and three fingers lay in a pool of blood.

Chapter Four

The Deadwood-Cheyenne stage run was an express with stops at Rapid Creek, Custer City, Indian Creek, Fort Laramie, Chugwater, Horse Creek and on into Cheyenne. Soiled Doves and gamblers made up the run's clientele, along with Chinamen and prospectors, single women looking for husbands, wives and children looking for their husbands and fathers, and actors and drummers looking for a place to ply their trades.

Kerlan had traveled out early in a rented buckboard to fetch Kate back to town. It was not an easy chore. Despite Kerlan's reassurances, Kate was somber and weighted down with guilt as Kerlan loaded her things in the wagon. Tom's drunken curses rang out crisply in the autumn air as the buckboard moved slowly away from the cabin and out on the main road.

They sat together over coffee at Sadie's. Kate was beginning to feel the stirring of freedom. Kerlan thought that time was all she needed to heal her terrible wound. El Patron Barela would treat her as a daughter, and the luxuries of the large hacienda near Taos would seem like heaven after her life of deprivation in the Black Hills.

"What are you going to do now, Sam?" questioned Kate. "Will I ever see you again?"

"I have a little business to take care of. After that I want to see what's left of my family. As for the future, I don't know what it will bring. I do hope to see you again, though, somewhere up the trail."

"Are you still in the same line of work?" she asked, hesitantly.

"Yes," he answered, quickly adding, "but I hope to make some changes soon."

Kerlan saw the disappointment on her face. Kate had never pressured Kerlan to leave his work behind, but he could always sense her disapproval.

The door opened and Catlin walked into the small eatery. He motioned to Kerlan and said, "The stage will be leaving in ten minutes." Kerlan nodded in thanks and turned back to Kate.

"I don't want to make much of a fuss out on the street. Nobody knows what is in the cards for themselves, but it is my hope that we will see each other again." Reaching into his coat he continued, "I've got an envelope here for you. My lawyer friend is meeting the stage in Cheyenne, and he'll take care of the paperwork on the divorce. He is also going to arrange for your travel down to New Mexico Territory. In the envelope is a sealed letter for Senor Barela and some money for the journey."

Tears welled up in Kate's eyes.

"Katie," Kerlan went on, "you're not to blame for what happened, but you are responsible for what happens from now on. You've got to forget the past couple of years and move on. You've got to be strong."

Kate nodded through the tears and wiped them from her face with a handkerchief. She cleared her throat and raised her chin. Kerlan knew that she would be just fine.

A small crowd gathered by the stage. A matronly lady stood wiping the face of a small boy. A young schoolmarm stood nervously beside a man Kerlan took to be some type of drummer. Kerlan hoped they would be good company for Kate on the long journey to Cheyenne.

The driver called for everyone to get aboard. Kate and Kerlan embraced discreetly; Kerlan helped her board the stage behind the mother and young child. The child smiled at Kate as they took their seats, and a small smile broke upon Kate's lips. It did Kerlan good to see it.

They held hands for a few moments through the stage window. As the driver readied the horses, Kerlan released his grip and stood back. The stage moved slowly forward. Kate raised her hand in goodbye. Kerlan answered by removing his hat as the stagecoach, pulled by six powerful horses, moved slowly out of Deadwood.

***

Kerlan walked over to the livery where Catlin was tying a load onto his pack horse. Kerlan saddled his roan and lead the animal to a hitching post outside the livery's office.

"I'm going to stop over at Mr. Drummond's office before we leave. Do you have everything I put on the list?" Kerlan asked.

"Yes sir," Catlin answered as he put the finishing touches on the pack saddles.

Kerlan picked up one of his horse's hooves and trimmed it with a pocket knife. He rubbed the roan's neck and spoke to it gently. Catlin watched with curiosity and then returned to his preparations.

Kerlan finished, looked over his horse and moved up the street to Drummond's office. Drummond was at the door when he saw Kerlan coming. He walked to meet him, and the two men sat together on a bench outside the assay office.

"What is your plan of action?" Drummond questioned in a dry, businesslike manner.

"I talked with Catlin about the last incident at Grizzly Bear Creek. We'll make for there and see if any signs of a trail can be found, but after three days I'm not hopeful. I made a list of your operations in the area and have a general idea of where the other miners and settlers are. I believe they'll strike again soon if they haven't already left the Hills. We'll travel the area and ask around. That's about all we can do."

"How do you intend to go about taking them?" Drummond asked, quickly losing his detached manner.

Kerlan paused and then said, "That depends how many there are of them, and how we come upon them, if we do."

From his curt reply, Drummond realized that Kerlan would divulge no more details.

"Well," Drummond concluded, "I wish you Godspeed. I'll be waiting to hear from you."

Drummond reached out his hand and received Kerlan's firm grasp. No more was said as the two walked away from one another.

Catlin was already seated on his horse as Kerlan returned to the livery stable. Kerlan again checked his tack and tightened up the cinch on the roan. He mounted the horse in a fluid motion, nodded once to Catlin, and began the journey he had told himself would be his last in this heavy and dreadful profession.

Chapter Five

Gil Stuart led his riders to the top of a rocky outcropping which hung like the bow of a ship over a small meadow. In the middle of the meadow beside a snake like stream stood a small line cabin, smoke rising from the thin pipe smokestack on the roof.

The leader of the gang took in the scene before him. He was a cautious man, made so by years of experience and a few tight situations that had taught him to observe, and then observe again.

He called back to Sanchez, a dark, heavy-set Mexican with a full beard and an aggressive manner, to ride down and check out the cabin. Sanchez grunted acceptance of the task and rode his stocky Texas pony down the rocky trail. He dismounted, at the same time drawing his pistol from its holster. Opening the door of the cabin, he carefully walked inside. He remained in the cabin for a short time before exiting, signaling to Stuart that all was clear.

Stuart gave the go-ahead to his men, who all eagerly cantered around him and down into the meadow. They had been in the saddle all day and were hungry for the deer Sanchez shot earlier along the trail. The men were also looking forward to the two bottles of whiskey Stuart had promised them after their long ride. Stuart would often let his men drink when he felt they were in a safe location, and after they had accomplished some goal. Small gestures like this seemed to keep them content and governable.

The men dismounted outside the cabin and made camp, going about their routine duties. Shelby Stuart, Gil's younger brother, and Jesse Siler handled the horses, unsaddling and finding them forage and water. Shelby assumed command when Gil wasn't available. Though his youth and impatience put the other men on edge, they accepted his authority because he was Gil's brother. Stuart demanded total dedication from his men, and the men followed him loyally because he was a natural leader and saw to their needs.

Stuart had been a young cavalry officer on the Confederate side in the Civil War. He had fought in a number of battles and received a leg wound at Shiloh which made him walk stiffly to this day. For this reason he liked to spend most of his time on horseback, a place he felt most comfortable since his cavalry days.

After the war he traveled back to Georgia to find his homeland destroyed and his people in despair. The news that Jefferson Davis was trying to form a new army drove him on to Texas. He found that to be a false hope, and instead joined with several other Confederates who took their revenge on the Yankees by stealing their horses and cattle. In the years to come, however, the stealing became more of a profession than a political statement. Stuart branched out into robbing stage coaches and small banks, and eventually a small gang formed around him. As the law became more diligent, Stuart came further west, working west Texas, New Mexico Territory and Nevada. He would work an area until things got a little too tight and then pull his gang out of the area and on to new territory. Due to this strategy, his gang was one of the last in the far West to remain intact. Yet Stuart could read the signs of the times, and knew that there were few prime areas left. Organized law enforcement and the courts were pecking away at this way of life.

In western Kansas, his gang was stealing horses when they ran into a posse in search of some bank robbers. Cursing his bad luck, Stuart narrowly escaped the posse, and moved his gang out of Kansas in a furious ride that wore out both men and horses. They camped in the Southern Black Hills for a number of weeks, living off the land and resting from their ordeal. But the men soon began to turn restless with this passive way of life, so Stuart moved them to the Northern Hills where they preyed on mining operations and ranches. Gathering the stolen horses and cattle, they returned with them to their hideout in the Southern Hills.

Stuart had chosen a meadow surrounded on three sides by sheer rock cliffs. Leaving one man to tend the livestock, Stuart and the remainder of the gang would conduct raids to add to their horses and cattle in this natural corral. Robbing the mining operations was gravy for the gang. Stuart had buried their money and gold dust near the corral. He entrusted its location only to his brother—just in case something would happen to him during one of the raids.

The gang was small: the Stuarts, Sanchez, a barely sixteen year old boy named Jesse Siler, and the Hufts, two German brothers.

Jesse Siler was a tall, silent boy who had joined the gang for adventure, and took pride in the men's acceptance of him as one of their own. Shelby Stuart had found Jesse in Cowles, New Mexico Territory, standing outside a saloon, looking like he had nowhere to go. Shelby asked him if he had a horse. Jesse nodded and had been with the gang ever since.

The Huft brothers were as different as two brothers could be. Gottlieb Huft, the older of the two, was a mean spirited German whom the other men avoided as much as possible. Gottlieb was fearless, often swearing at the gang members in his native tongue. He listened only to Gil Stuart. For his part Stuart put up with the bad-tempered German because Gottlieb was undaunted in a fight, a man you would want at your side if you were backed into a corner.

Reinhold, gentle and friendly, was just the opposite of his troublesome brother. He loved animals, serving as the horse doctor of the gang. Stuart tried to separate the brothers as much as he could, for Gottlieb was especially hard on Reinhold, taunting him and calling him names in their native tongue. Stuart would leave Reinhold behind to watch the livestock when the gang went raiding; the other men secretly wished he would leave that task to Gottlieb.

Stuart rode his horse down to the cabin in the meadow. Sanchez was readying the fire for the venison, and the boys were watering the horses in the creek. Gottlieb was rummaging around in the cabin and came out the door as Stuart rode up. Stuart dismounted and called for Jesse to unsaddle his horse and get it some water and feed. He removed his saddle bag and entered the cabin. Inside were three bunks, a small pot-bellied stove, and a large stump which served as a table, surrounded by three smaller stumps used as chairs. He laid the saddle bag on the large stump and pulled from it a bottle of whiskey, handing it to Gottlieb as he entered the cabin behind him. Gottlieb grunted something in German and quickly left. Stuart pulled another bottle from the bag and pulled the cork from it with his teeth. He sat down on one of the bunks and took a long drink from the bottle. He set the bottle on the large stump and massaged his stiff leg. The sweet smell of roasting venison entered the cabin, and Stuart leaned back against the wall and began to plan the next day's raid.

They had been in the Hills for four months. During that time they had gathered a substantial number of cattle and had enlarged the remuda. Stuart was now beginning to believe that it was time for he and his men to move on, driving the animals south and selling them. The cool nights of the Black Hills were a foreboding of winter, and made Stuart yearn for a warmer climate, perhaps Arizona Territory or the border towns of Mexico.

Earlier in the week he and Sanchez had scouted out a ranch in the lower Hills on French Creek. The rancher was raising a fine string of horses. It was a small operation, perhaps two or three men, and it would be easy pickens for Stuart and his gang. He would head out tomorrow with everyone except Reinhold, gather up the animals and bring them back to camp. They would then lay low for a week in order to rest up, and then move south and out of Dakota Territory for good.

Shelby Stuart came into the cabin, grabbed the bottle out of his brother's hands and stretched out on the other bunk. He took a long drink of whiskey and let go a sigh of satisfaction.

"What are the boys up to?" Gil asked, less out of interest than from a sense of duty.

"Oh, Gottlieb is giving Reiny hell and Sanchez is cooking the deer. Jesse is fixin' some tack."

Shelby was many years younger than Gil. When their mother died in Georgia, he had been sent out to Gil by an uncle. He was a dark, strong young man with brown hair and an impatience his brother could not understand. The war had taught Gil Stuart to be patient and to recognize the limitations of men, but his less experienced brother was quick tempered and intolerant. He liked to command but had not earned the respect of the other men. This made him all the more aggressive. Gil cared deeply for his little brother and could overlook his flaws. He felt an obligation for the young man who had never known their father.

"What's the plan?" Shelby asked Gil.

The plan was always Gil's burden. The men ate, drank, and slept with no more thought about tomorrow than the horses had. It was always he who had to think and worry, to plan and provide.

"I'm thinking of heading south. We'll hit that ranch Sanchez and I scouted and then come back here to regroup. In a week to ten days we'll drive them south and sell them."

"Good," Shelby responded. "These cold nights are starting to get to me. This ol' boy from Georgia wants to feel the sun on his face."

A knock was heard at the door and Jesse Siler entered the cabin. He was a polite and quiet boy, tall and thin with curly black hair and a high sing-song voice.

"Sanchez sez that the venison is ready, Mr. Stuart."

"Thanks, boy, how are those horses lookin'?"

Jesse always felt honored when Gil Stuart spoke directly to him.

"They're doing good, sir. Reiny took a stone out of a hoof of Gottlieb's mare. The horses seem to be holdin' up good."

"That's fine Jess. You tell Reiny to have them ready for a long ride tomorrow. Now, boys, let's have some supper."

***

Catlin sat before the small fire enclosed by a border of rocks. The cool night was the second he would have to endure without company. Kerlan had set out alone on the second day of their journey. He told Catlin to head south-southwest and that he would return to meet him in two or three day's time. Catlin didn't relish the thought of another night alone in the Hills. He sat trying to warm himself as he poured another cup of strong black coffee; he felt a presence to his left near a stand of small pine trees. As he turned his head quickly a steady voice broke the stillness of the lonely night.

"Sorry to come up on you this way, Catlin."

Sam Kerlan stepped into the fires quivering light. "I believe it would be best we put that fire out, but not before I have a cup of that coffee."

"Mr. Kerlan," answered a shaken Catlin, "I reckon you spooked me a bit. I sort of expected you to come back in daylight."

Kerlan came to the side of the fire and poured a cup. After taking several short gulps, he returned his attention to Catlin.

"I found where the Stuart gang is holing up; a small canyon thirty miles south of here. They've gathered up a respectable herd of cattle and a bunch of horses."

"How many of them are there?" questioned Catlin.

"I only saw one man. The rest of the gang must be out on a raid. From the size of the herd they will be moving out soon."

Kerlan took another drink and splashed the remainder into the fire. Smoke swirled in the air, and it seemed as if a lamp had been blown out in a room. Red embers continued to burn brightly in the stone enclosure.

"What do you plan to do?" ventured Catlin.

"Well," Kerlan came back slowly, not used to sharing his plans with anyone, "tomorrow we'll make toward their camp and secure ourselves above it. Then we'll wait and get a better idea of how many men there are. From the tracks going in and out of the place I would guess five to seven."

Kerlan did not explain further. Catlin realized that only when he knew the exact numbers they were facing would Kerlan then decide on a plan of action.

"I'm going to see to my horse. We'd better get some sleep. It'll be a long ride tomorrow."

As Kerlan walked away from the fire's red glow, Catlin laid out his bed roll and made himself as comfortable as possible. Looking up into the night sky, he wondered what the next day would bring.

Chapter Six

Reinhold drew placidly on his pipe as he watched the other men prepare their mounts for the day's raid. He looked forward to being alone with the animals and with his own thoughts. As early as he could remember, he had felt a certain affinity with horses and cattle, dogs and cats, wild animals and tame.

He felt certain he would settle down soon. He had carefully saved his money over the last few years, gathering a stake so he could set up a place of his own. His main desire was to be alone and, in particular, to be shed of his brother Gottlieb. He was sick of his brother's cruelty to him, the gang, and to the animals; Gottlieb treated animals in the same harsh manner he treated humans. Reinhold could never understand how a man could beat a horse into submission. A good horse was like a partner, something to be nurtured and seen to, trusted and made better. There was no love lost between the brothers, and Reinhold longed for the day that would be their last together.

Stuart secured his saddle and looked over the men. He was anxious to get started on this frosty morning. He knew that this would be the last raid in the Hills, and that he would be leading the men down to the plains as soon as they secured the last bunch of horses. They would rest for a time and be on their way.

Gottlieb was swearing under his breath in guttural German. Sanchez was rolling a cigarette while sitting calmly in his saddle. The boys rode up from the creek in a slow canter and came to a stop by the cabin.

"All ready, Mr. Stuart," Jesse said earnestly.

"How long will this one take, Gil?" asked Shelby.

"We should be back late tomorrow," answered Stuart. "I want to get this one done quickly and get back to camp. In a week we'll be in Nebraska."

"Mount up, Gott! Take care of the stock, Reiny. Be sure to see to that dun mare."

Stuart and Gottlieb swung up into their saddles. The gang loped up past the protruding rock face and out of the serene little canyon.

***

The two riders kept a steady pace throughout the day. Catlin, because of his work for Drummond, was used to spending long days in the saddle. Kerlan was impressed with his ability to stay abreast.

It was early evening when they stopped to rest, water the horses, and have a meal of hardtack, cold beans and jerky.

"We're close now," Kerlan said matter-of-factly, as if speaking to himself. He picked up a stick from the ground and cleared an area of brush with his boot. He drew what looked to Catlin like the mantle of a gas lamp.

"The canyon is closed at one end which makes it perfect for holding livestock. At the open end there's an outcropping of rock. I want you to place yourself at the closed end of the canyon. We'll find you a secure spot where you can place some rifle shots. I'm going to move to, and dig in, at the rock face near the opening. At my signal you'll begin firing as rapidly as possible. Between rifle shots fire your pistol. This will make them believe that several men are attacking from that direction."

"But that means you'll have to face the whole gang at the opening," Catlin said, concerned.

"Not if you shoot a couple of them," Kerlan said with a wry smile.

"Do you think they're all there now?" asked Catlin.

"We won't know till morning. I'll work you around to the closed end, and we'll wait there and keep a watch on things. If they're in place in the morning, I'll move around to the rock face. If not, we'll wait till they're gathered. Remember, the important thing is to let them believe that you're more than one man."

Catlin nodded understanding and took another bite of jerky. Kerlan walked to the stream and took several gulps from a cupped hand. He then filled his canteen and tied it on the saddle. He swung up onto his horse and spoke again to Catlin.

"We've gotta be quiet from this point on. Any questions on the plan?"

"No sir," answered Catlin.

"O.K.," Kerlan said looking into the evening's dimming light, "let's move to the rim."

Chapter Seven

"Snub him up," Louis LeBeau said to his younger brother. "Don't let him come up on ya."

Andy pulled the horse tight to the tethering post. The animal tried to move first one way and then another but finally realized he was stuck in one spot.

"Leave him tied for awhile before we put the saddle on," Louis explained to his brother. "It sort of tires them out a little."

"How's it going, boys?" Joe Hoskins yelled from the corral lean-to.

Louis waved a signal that all was well and went back to work on the horses. The LeBeau boys had been with Hoskins since Louis was twelve and little Andy nine. The boys were half French and half Sioux and had grown into handsome young men with high foreheads and curly black hair. Louis was now seventeen and had become a proficient horse trainer. Andy, who wished to follow in his older brother's footsteps, also had potential with horses.

Hoskins came by the boys after a cattle drive to the Pine Ridge Reservation for the annual slaughter. Hoskins had hired on their father as a drover and had allowed the boys to tag along. The elder Lebeau's horse had taken a hole and came over on him, killing both horse and rider instantly. Hoskins took in the two youngsters and in time, the two looked to him as a father.

Hoskins had come up from Texas during the late drives and had settled in the lower Hills. He raised cattle and horses, never on a large scale, but of such quality that people sought him out. He and the boys had built a good life along the banks of French Creek. They didn't need much as the Hills were rich in game and firewood.

"Louis," Joe called. "Send Andy over here."

Louis gestured to his brother and continued his work with the horses. Andy walked over to the lean-to and raised his eyebrows in an inquiring manner.

"We're getting a might low on venison, Andy," Joe said, tying off a new halter. "Take the Winchester and see if you can shoot one for the salt locker. Try for a doe if you can, always better meat."

Andy eagerly acknowledged the instructions. He loved to hunt and was proud that Hoskins trusted him to go out alone.

He went to the big corral and saddled up his paint. He tied her off at the lean-to and went into the cabin to fetch the Winchester. He stuffed it into the leather scabbard and tied it onto his saddle. In a single easy motion he was on his horse.

"You be careful now," Joe said, "and don't be out more than a few hours. Three shots in the air will bring us to you. Good luck, boy."

Andy smiled a wide, pleased smile and trotted out of the yard. Joe watched after him and smiled to himself.

***

Andy Lebeau leaned the heavy rifle over the saddle's cantle and looked down the sights at a deer grazing in the open meadow. The deer bolted just as he was ready to pull the trigger. Andy couldn't figure out what had scared the deer off. He put the rifle in the scabbard and mounted his horse.

He rode across the meadow at a slight canter, enjoying the gentle movement of the horse beneath him. Like his brother, he was a natural horseman, seemingly born to the saddle.

At the other side of the grassy expanse he coaxed his horse up a rise to get a better vantage point. Halfway up his horse stopped abruptly in its tracks, throwing Andy forward in the saddle. Righting his balance he looked up to see a fat, bearded man staring down at him from the top of the hill.

"Where you going, Mijo?" demanded Sanchez in a menacing tone.

Andy was an open and trusting young man, but there was something in the Mexican's voice that put him on his guard. He didn't answer the man, instead turning his pony sharply and galloping down the rise.

Sanchez rode after him and quickly caught up to the boy in the center of the meadow. Wishing to stop the boy, the Mexican took his bullwhip and struck him several times on his back and head. Andy held tight to his reins and for a time managed to draw away from his pursuer. Beating his small Texas cowpony with the whip, Sanchez again caught up to the boy. He drew in close to the front quarter of Andy's paint and began forcing the horse to turn into a pile of bunched up logs. Andy urged his horse to jump, but the terrified pony was off balance and galloped straight into the fallen timbers, falling head forward over onto its back.

Sanchez slowed and turned, trotting back to the place where the boy and his horse had fallen. The pony stood dazed next to the boy lying, as if resting, on his back in the heavy grass. The Mexican dismounted and walked over. No stranger to death, Sanchez knew immediately that the boy was gone. Grabbing the body by the back of the collar, he dragged the lifeless boy over to his still benumbed horse. He draped the boy's body over the saddle. Taking out his knife, Sanchez cut one of the reins off the bridle and used it to tie one of the dead boy's hands to his boot under the belly of the horse. Sanchez took the other rein and led the little paint over to his own horse. He checked his cinch and mounted. Pulling his sombrero tightly down upon his head, he kicked his horse into a trot and led the paint with its bouncing, lifeless cargo out of the meadow.

***

Gil Stuart drew on a hand-rolled cigarette as he stood on the top of a knoll waiting for the return of Sanchez. In the distance he saw two horses coming toward him. He watched closely until he discerned that only the lead horse had a rider. Further scrutiny confirmed that the rider was Sanchez.

He walked down the small hill to where the other men were gathered.

"Sanchez is coming and he's leading a horse. Mount up!"

The men reacted quickly to Stuart's command and in a moment were riding at full canter behind him.

As they rode up to Sanchez, Stuart now saw the body on the back of the paint horse. He dismounted and walked over to the paint. Grabbing the boy's head by the hair, he pulled it up to get a full look at the face.

"He's one of the boys from the horse camp," Stuart said as he dropped the boy's head against the horse's side. "Was he alone?"

"Si, the niño was out hunting," answered Sanchez, matter-of-factly.

Long used to violence and death, Stuart had no need to know the details. He just needed to take care of this inconvenience. He took a knife out of his boot and cut the bridle strap, and the boy slid slowly off the saddle and onto the ground.

"Shelby," ordered Stuart, "you and Jesse take him over and put some rocks on him. Sanchez, you ride ahead and scout out the horse camp but wait for us. We'll ride in together."

The youngest members of the gang dismounted and walked over to where the boy was lying. They each grabbed a boot and dragged the body away from the party of men and down a small gully. Shelby first went through the boy's clothes, finding only a small silver cross which he tore from around his neck. They then covered the body with rocks. As Shelby walked back toward the horses, Jesse paused to say a prayer over the boy's impromptu grave.

***

They tied the horses off in a pine thicket well away from the meadow's rim. Kerlan took a bundle down from the pack horse and unrolled it onto the ground. Wrapped in an oilcloth were a .44 Henry and a sawed-off scattergun. Taking both guns and a supply of ammunition, he said to Catlin, "Bring plenty of shells. We're going to find a secure enough place for you so that even if things go wrong at my end of the canyon, you'll be able to hold them off with your Sharps until they get bored and leave you alone."

Catlin poured several more handfuls of rifle cartridges into his game bag. Instead of feeling fretful, he felt strangely settled about the coming action. He hadn't known Kerlan more than a week, but already felt perfectly confident in his calm companion's abilities. He had seen Kerlan draw his pistol only once, but on that occasion the action had been so quick and sure that it had erased any doubts in Catlin's mind.

Kerlan watched Catlin make his final preparations. When Catlin was finished he looked up and met Kerlan's steady gaze. Kerlan nodded and Catlin followed him down the dark trail.

Kerlan had scouted out the area the day before and knew how he would place his rifleman. At the bottom of the closed end of the canyon lay a bed of loose rock and pine seedlings. This led up to a gathering of large boulders whose backdrop was a sheer rock face. From here a competent rifleman could hold off thirty men. Kerlan knew that if he were killed or disabled at the other end of the canyon, the Stuart gang would not waste time trying to dislodge the lone rifleman, but would focus on gathering their livestock and making their escape.

The two men moved to the rim and down to the boulders. From this vantage point they could see the figure of a man sitting close by a fire near the small cabin. They saw cattle and horses moving about, and could hear a stream in the distance. Kerlan set his rifle and scattergun down and began to prepare for a long night of vigilance.

"You take the first watch. Be sure to wake me if there's any change at all down there."

Catlin nodded his acknowledgement and leaned his rifle against a large rock. As he watched the unknown man down in the valley, he wondered what fate had in store for this stranger, for himself, and for Kerlan.

***

No shots were heard all afternoon at the horse camp on French Creek. Hoskins figured Andy must be having a run of bad luck. It was getting late in the day, and Hoskins was just beginning to worry.

He and Louis were trimming hooves near the barn when something caught Louis' eye. He tapped Hoskins on the shoulder and pointed up the creek. Hoskins saw several men riding toward them. They were moving at a slow pace. Hoskins thought they were most likely a cattle outfit looking for a few head to replenish their remuda. Just to be on the safe side, Hoskins gestured to Louis to go in and get the rifles.

The small band of men entered the yard and rode up to the horsemen. Stuart waived a greeting and Hoskins nodded in response.

"Howdy," greeted Stuart. "I hear tell you gentlemen might have some horseflesh for sale."

"Yes, sir," answered Hoskins, "we have a few head that ain't promised to nobody."

"Good," continued Stuart. "Mind if we get down? We've spent awhile in the saddle on our way here."

"No, no, get down and rest up. I'll have Louis tend to your horses and I'll put on a pot of coffee and get your boys something to eat."

"Mighty kind of you," said Stuart as he and his men dismounted. Louis took the reins from each man and led the horses down to the creek.

"You didn't see a boy riding a spotted pony on your way in? I sent him out for some meat, and he should have been back by now."

"No, can't say we did," Stuart answered convincingly. "He probably shot a big one and is having trouble getting it home."

"Yea, that's more than likely what happened. So, you want some horses."

"We need twenty to thirty head. We're on a drive to Montana and reckon we'll need to replace some mounts."

"Well," mused Hoskins, "I believe I could let you have fifteen or twenty. Most of my horses are committed to the cavalry at Fort Meade. I have a yearly contract to fill for them."

The answer took Stuart aback. To take horses earmarked for the U.S. Cavalry was risky even for him. All the more reason to leave the Hills and go south after this last run.

"We'll take whatever you can spare," said Stuart.

Hoskins left the group of men and went into the cabin to start a fire for the coffee. The men walked over and gathered around Stuart.

"Gottlieb," Stuart directed, "you take care of the old man in the cabin. Sanchez, you the boy. No gunfire if you can help it. We don't want to disturb the horses. Shelby and Jesse, you go start a head count."

Stuart began to roll a cigarette as he watched his men go off to their appointed tasks. He regretted ordering the deaths of the old man and the boy, but hard experience had taught him what happens when a witness is left to tell the tale. In Arizona Territory Stuart had been working with a small group of banditos on the border, when they robbed a small bank in Nogales. During the hold-up, one of the men let slip the location where they were to meet to split the money. One of the clerks overheard this exchange, and a few hours after the men had settled into their hideout they were attacked by a large posse. Stuart barely escaped with his life, and from that day took a cold view of living witnesses.

Hoskins was leaning over the small pot bellied stove when Gottlieb entered the cabin. He looked up and smiled.

"I'll have some hot coffee ready soon. Where are you boys out of?"

"Texas," Gottlieb responded in a guttural tone.

"You German?" asked Hoskins. "I worked with some Germans on a drive once. Hard working fellers."

Hoskins began to blow on the small pile of kindling in the stove as Gottlieb moved across the cabin and stood over him.

"Yep," continued Hoskins as he worked the kindling into a small flame, "those fellas put in long days and had big appetites. That's what I remember about them."

Gottlieb removed a bowie knife from his belt and stood for a moment behind his unsuspecting host. Drawing it back in an underarm motion, he drove it solidly into the lower back of Hoskins. Just as quickly he drew it out. Hoskins fell for a moment against the stove whose flame was reaching a crescendo. He used the stove for support to stand to full height and turned to look at his assailant who had now stepped back. A look of bewilderment was on the wounded man's face as he stood with open mouth before the burly German.

"Wh...wh...Why?" This was all that he could draw from the depth of his soul as he fell full length onto the dirt floor of the cabin.

Sanchez moved casually to the edge of French Creek where Louis LeBeau was watering the horses. He pulled out a plug of tobacco and bit down on a generous chaw. He offered Louis a bite but the boy refused.

"You like the caballos, Mijo?" Sanchez questioned in broken Tex-Mex English.

The boy nodded and continued with his work. Sanchez walked over to his horse and took from its saddlebag a length of leather rope. He returned to the boy who was checking the back hoof of Stuart's horse.

"I show you how to make a Mexican hackamore," Sanchez said grinning ominously through rotten teeth.

"I know how to make a hackamore," the boy answered, not disrespectfully.

"A 'Mexican' hackamore," said Sanchez angrily and began to fashion the leather into a configuration. Louis watched the Mexican at work, at first warily, but then with genuine curiosity as the rope work took some intriguing shapes. Louis couldn't figure out how those twists and knots would ultimately end up a hackamore.

"That's a strange piece of tack," Louis said trying to appease Sanchez's evident irritation. "What's it used for?"

"To squeeze the life out of a little, halfbreed Nino," said Sanchez as he threw the open noose around Louis' neck and drew it tight. He pulled and led the boy away from the creek. Sanchez drew in the slack until the boy was on his knees before him. Louis' hands were about his neck, desperately trying to loosen the rope's constricting grasp. Sanchez walked around behind the boy and turned his back to him. He drew up the rope over his shoulder until Louis was back to back with him. The Mexican pulled the rope further until Louis' feet were off the ground and the back of his head was on Sanchez's shoulder. The Mexican stood still as the boy's arms and legs flailed wildly in the air. Louis gasped for air, but none could enter his lungs through his now closed windpipe. Sanchez shook his shoulders to speed up the process. The boy made a few last movements and then hung limply on the Mexican's back like suspended game.

Sanchez stood still for a moment to be sure the job was done. He let the rope slide slowly down, and the boy slipped gently down to earth, first on his knees, then to a sitting position from which he rolled peacefully onto his side. The Mexican removed the noose from Louis' neck, untied the slipknot, rolled it up and returned it to his saddle bag. He walked back to the boy and turned him onto his back. He removed spurs, four silver dollars from his pocket, and tore the silver cross from his neck. Using his boot, he then pushed the boy over on his stomach and grasped him easily by his belt and collar. Sanchez dragged the body into the creek, releasing the boy when he reached the middle where the waters moved steadily. Louis' body moved slowly down stream, turning completely over once, exposing the proud, high forehead one last time to the sky over the boy's beloved Black Hills.

Stuart was drawing on his second cigarette when first Gottlieb and then Sanchez returned to him. He knew by their silence that their tasks were completed. Moments later Shelby and Jesse rode up.

"We counted 50 to 60 head," called out Shelby. "Nice stock!"

Tossing his cigarette to the ground, Stuart surveyed the area. "We'll camp here for the night and move out early in the morning. Sanchez, you start up some fix'ins for supper. You boys look around for anything we might need and, Gottlieb, you come with me. I want to take a look at those horses."

A heavy wind moved through the pines and scented the air in the meadow. The horses sensed the heavy atmosphere of death and moved uneasily in the corral. Several trout, lingering lazily downstream by a large rock, darted off quickly as a dark figure passed in the water above them.

Chapter Eight

Reinhold Huft sat on the front porch of the cabin listening to the nearby stream and puffing complacently on his pipe. It was dusk, and the livestock had settled down on the cool fall evening. Reinhold stared up at the stars and thought of the future. This was how he wanted to live his life. He wanted to work long, peaceful days with his animals and then settle down in the quiet evenings, listening to the sound of moving water. He was happiest when he was alone. Reinhold did not dislike people, but felt in general that they made too many demands on him, always seeming to want something of his: His time, his money, or his peace of mind.

Reinhold was thinking of the future. A short time back he had decided that this would be his last year with the Stuart gang. He looked up to Gil Stuart, who had always treated him with consideration and had been his protector against the excesses of Gottlieb. But it was time to move on.

Reinhold didn't hate Gottlieb. He didn't hate anyone, for it was not in his nature. He just could not understand Gottlieb's cruelty and how he treated people and animals. He was convinced that his happiness in this world meant getting away from his brother.

While the gang was busy robbing small banks over the years, Reinhold was equally busy depositing his share in the larger banks he came across during their travels. He had money in Denver, Cheyenne, Santa Fe, and a few smaller towns. All told he had a hefty sum saved away. He would soon collect his money and settle down on his own place to live out his dream.

On the cliff above the day-dreaming German, another man was considering his future. Catlin sat in silence, listening to the sounds of the night. He was thinking about Deadwood and of Suzi Wong, the prostitute he visited often in the Chinese section of the town. Suzi was young and beautiful and Catlin was in love with her. Suzi treated him coolly, like any other paying customer, but Catlin looked on her differently. He dreamed of Suzi long after the short, furious paid-for trysts were over. Once, he had asked her to marry him, but she pretended to not understand what he was saying. She had other customers waiting.

Kerlan stirred in his sleep and startled Catlin out of his pleasant thoughts. He looked down into the canyon and could see the embers of a dying fire. The man in the cabin had turned in, and all Catlin could hear was the distant flow of water and an occasional horse whinny.

Kerlan awoke and stood to stretch. He also looked carefully down into the canyon. Turning to Catlin he said in a whisper, "You try and get some sleep. I figure they'll be here in the morning, and we both better have our wits about us."

Catlin nodded in agreement and turned onto his side. His thoughts returned to Suzi, and when he fell asleep his face wore a pleased smile.

Kerlan wished he could smoke a cheroot but knew the scent would startle the horses down in the canyon. As he sat leaning against a boulder, his thoughts also turned to a woman. Kate would be arriving in Cheyenne tomorrow evening. His lawyer friend, Bill Torrence, would have everything ready for her and in a couple of days would send her on her way to New Mexico. All would be well for Kate, at least for a time. Kerlan thought for a moment of their possible future together. He chased the thought off, unwilling to risk the pain of another separation. Kate's leaving him was a deep wound, and time had not healed it. Kerlan told himself that his arrangements for Kate were done out of pity and a responsibility to a lost love. But occasionally he allowed himself to wonder if his true motivation was actually a deep love that had never truly died.

***

The sound of men's voices and horses' hooves brought Catlin out of a deep sleep into an upright sitting position. Kerlan, peering down into the canyon, glanced back as Catlin awoke and waved him to silence.

Gil Stuart and his men were moving their newly acquired horses and cattle into the canyon. The men were yelling and waving their hats and ropes in the air as the livestock moved ahead of them.

Reinhold opened up the makeshift gate and the animals entered swiftly to join the already established herd. Taking advantage of the sudden commotion, Kerlan quickly spoke to Catlin.

"We'll let them settle in for a couple of hours. When I feel the time is right, I'll move around to the rock face. I'll be out of range so when I get set I'll fire a few shots in the air. That's your signal to place a few good rounds. If you can take one out, that would be helpful. Two would be great. My guess is that they'll think they're surrounded and make for the open end. Remember to shoot quickly to make it appear there's more than one of you up here. Any questions?"

As Catlin shook his head, Kerlan realized how much he valued this new partner who listened and agreed to his part of the bargain without questions and second guesses.

***

Reinhold greeted Stuart as he rode up to the cabin. Anticipating their early return, Reinhold had prepared a large pot of stew. Its aroma made the boys glad their job was done.

Before he let the men settle down to eat and relax, Stuart had Reinhold and Jesse enter the corral. He knew there would be some commotion as the two groups of horses struggled to establish a new pecking order. The presence of humans seemed to bring calm and order to these inevitable dominance rituals.

Stuart told Gottlieb and Shelby to turn the old mounts in and saddle up fresh horses, a practice learned from his cavalry days. He always had fresh mounts at the ready in case of the need for a quick escape.

After the work was completed, the men settled down to Reinhold's stew. Reinhold was a fair cook and creatively utilized whatever was available to him. To this particular stew he had added wild mushrooms and asparagus along with some potatoes and onions the boys found in a ranch garden after one of their recent raids.

The men enjoyed their meal and afterward were free to go about their own pursuits. Sanchez went into the cabin for a mid-day siesta, while Gottlieb grabbed a plate and went down to the creek to pan for gold. The boys grabbed their ropes and went out to the meadow to best one another with rope throws. Gil Stuart stretched out under a tree near the cabin, and Reinhold went about clearing up after the meal.

Kerlan and Catlin watched these routine movements from their perch high above the canyon floor. Kerlan gave the men in the meadow time to settle into their mid-day activities, and then motioned to Catlin that he would begin his slow journey around the rim of the canyon to his position at the open end.

Within an hour, Kerlan had traveled the circumference of the canyon. He would now have to make a final run across a wide expanse to reach the rock face. Looking back at the cabin, he saw the men still in their previous positions; only the cook was now watching the boys lasso a stump.

Kerlan made his move to the rock face. From the other side of the canyon Catlin could see his dash. He knew that soon the fight would commence.

Reaching the outcropping, Kerlan glanced down to see if he had been spotted. There was no change in the activity of the men, however, so he continued on, climbing to the top of the rock face. Peering over the edge he noticed a pile of rocks with a number of small seedlings protruding from amongst them. The site wouldn't protect him from bullets, but it would give him the element of surprise if, and when, the men made their way out of the canyon. The success of Kerlan's whole plan hinged on convincing the Stuart gang that there were a number of men at the closed end with Catlin.

He paused for a few minutes, readying his firearms. He drew a long breath, raised his pistol, and fired it into the air.

When Catlin heard two quick pistol shots, he leveled and fired his Sharps Carbine. Gottlieb was crouching by the creek, and Catlin's second round caught him square in the back, causing him to fall forward into the stream. Gottlieb instinctively forced himself first to his knees and then to his full height, pulling his pistol from its holster and firing wildly in no particular direction. He stumbled across the stream, continuing to fire his pistol. By the time he crossed the water, his Colt was empty, but still he continued automatically to pull back the hammer and squeeze the trigger. Several clicks could be heard before he finally seized up and fell forward onto the rocks of the river bank.

After shooting the tall man, Catlin quickly trained his Sharps on the others. When they heard the first rounds, the boys and Reinhold ran to the cabin where Gil Stuart and Sanchez were taking cover.

Catlin continued his shooting, using the pistol between rifle shots to create the impression that several gunmen were shooting from the closed end. Although the gang was now safely out of harm's way behind the cabin, the men were confused and feeling trapped.

"They shot Gott!" yelled Jesse in a panic.

"Forget Gott," Stuart commanded, struggling to regain control of the situation. "Sanchez, you and Reiny bring the horses around to this side of the cabin. Shelby and I will cover you."

With no hesitation at all, the Mexican and German ran around the cabin and across an open area to untie the horses from a hitching post, while Shelby and Gil fired in the direction from which they believed the shooting originated. Catlin fired his rifle at the two men leading the horses, and one bullet struck Reinhold. As he fell he held out the reins to Sanchez. The Mexican grabbed them and pulled the horses behind the cabin.

The gunfire was causing havoc in the corral, and in a flood of animal flesh, the horses and cattle broke down the fence and stampeded in a crazed manner toward the canyon opening. Gil Stuart saw this as their chance for escape and ordered the boys to mount up and follow the animals out of the canyon. Shelby and Sanchez got on their horses while Jesse held Stuart's for him.

"Get up boy, and ride like hell." Stuart yelled. "Look out for yourself."

Mounted, the men spurred their horses after the rampaging livestock. Catlin continued his fire, without results; quickly the men were getting out of range and he had never been proficient with a moving target. A last lucky shot, however, grazed Gil Stuart's arm and embedded itself in his horse's neck. The animal crumpled to the ground, throwing Stuart in front of it. Sanchez, riding behind Stuart, reached down quickly and pulled his boss up on the back of his Texas cow pony.

Shelby and Jesse, riding out front nearer the rock face, felt freedom within their grasp when Kerlan stood up from the small cluster of pines. A Colt in each hand, he fired on the approaching horsemen.

Jesse caught a round full in the chest and fell off the back of his horse as if pulled by a rope tied around his waist to a tree. Shelby Stuart was dead before he left the saddle with bullet holes in his throat and square in the center of his forehead.

Sanchez was still far enough away from this action at the rock face to avoid it. He whirled his little cow pony in a close circle and made for the rise at the open end of the meadow. Screaming in a high pitched tone, he exhorted the little Texas pony, burdened with two men, to climb the rise with every ounce of strength it had. Kerlan and Catlin both tried rifle shots, but by this time the two men were well out of range.

Kerlan made his way down from the rock face to the bodies of the two men he had killed. He was startled by their youth and shook his head in disgust. Kerlan's work had pitted him against men and boys from fifteen to fifty, but pangs of guilt still entered the recesses of his soul when he was forced to kill youngsters.

He walked to the creek where the body of a huge man lay. He had been shot in the back and the bullet had passed clean through. The cattle and horses had trampled him on their frantic race out of the meadow and his features were distorted beyond recognition.

Moaning could now be heard, and he looked up to see Catlin leaning over a wounded man by the cabin. Reaching them he informed Catlin, "Two got away. From the looks of things one of them was Stuart. Let's get this one into the cabin and look after his wound."

They carried Reinhold into the cabin and laid him on one of the bunks. Kerlan opened the man's coat and shirt to examine the wound. The bullet had hit him in the side but at such a trajectory that it had glanced off his ribs. The man would live.

"Dress the wound and I'll gather up the dead," Kerlan said as he walked toward the door. Turning, he said, "By the way, Catlin, you did a good job out there this morning."

"Thanks, Mr. Kerlan. I just wish we would have gotten the other two. I don't think Mr. Drummond will be too pleased with all this."

"Drummond needn't worry. Stuart was shot up, and if he lives, he'll high tail it out of these parts. He stayed just a little too long in these hills."

Chapter Nine

The dead were secured over the backs of horses, the big man on a single horse and the two youngsters together on a lone mount. The unpleasant task finished, Kerlan lit up a cheroot and stood near the stream.

The door of the cabin opened, and Catlin stepped out in the midmorning sun. He noticed Kerlan and walked to meet him.

"The fella's talking a bit. Seems kinda nice. You know, I didn't see him pick up a gun through the whole fight."

Blowing out cigar smoke Kerlan responded, "I'll go in and talk with him."

Inside the cabin Reinhold lay on his back, pain shooting through his side when he breathed too heavily. Kerlan entered the small room and looked down at the German, not in an unfriendly manner.

"How ya doing," Kerlan asked.

"Goot, very goot, tank you," responded Reinhold. "My ribs pain me a bit, not too bad. Is everyone dead?"

"Two young'uns and a big fella," answered Kerlan.

"Dat would be Shelby and Jesse. Poor boys. Und mah broder, Gottlieb. His soul be in hell by now."

"Two others escaped."

"Yah, dat would be Mr. Stuart and Sanchez."

"My partner says you didn't pick up a gun through it all. Why?"

"I am not a gunman. I am a stockman. I work the horses for Mr. Stuart."

"I see. Will you be able to travel? We need to get back to Deadwood as soon as possible."

"Yah, Deadwood," Reinhold said sadly. "Yah, I can travel."

"What I meant to say is, well, can you travel by yourself? As far as I'm concerned you're free to go. I would only suggest you find better people to work for."

"Oh, sir, tank you, tank you. Yah, Yah, I will never work for Mr. Stuart again. I will work for Reinhold Huft, mineself, from now on. Tank you, sir, tank you."

After shaking the German's outstretched hand, Kerlan turned and left the cabin. Catlin was readying the horses for the journey north, and Kerlan looked over the canyon one last time. Would a different plan have produced a better outcome? But perhaps if things had been different, the good brother would now be dead and the bad one still breathing. Kerlan quickly drove these thoughts out of his head—he had no desire to waste time wondering about events that were now past.

Up in their saddles the two men looked at one another. They'd been through much together on this cool autumn day. But they would not speak about their experiences. Few real warriors feel the need to speak of their trials and triumphs. They had lived it, and that was enough.

Kerlan led the way with Catlin at the drags; between the two of them rode their lifeless cargo.

Chapter Ten

They traveled north into the evening and throughout the night. Kerlan was eager to get back to Deadwood in order to dispose of the dead properly. The two didn't say much on the ride, keeping to their own thoughts. Catlin's mind was filled with Suzie Wong, and how he would go to her as soon as he arrived back in town. Kerlan, on the other hand, was pondering his more distant future. For years now, some unfinished business had been weighing heavily on Kerlan's mind. On this trip back to Deadwood, it became more than rumination. It became a decision.

The steep mountain trail led down into a canyon and on to an open meadow where a trading post was set up. Smoke rose from the chimney pipe of the dingy little cabin. Two horses were tied to the hitchin' post outside, and voices could be heard from within.

"Hello the post," Kerlan said loudly as they approached.

A thin old man with a dirty apron came out the door, followed by two young cowboys. The old man stared at the new arrivals and said through a toothless grin, "Howdy, welcome to Smith's Post. Climb down and I'll fix ya' up with some vittles and coffee."

Then, catching sight of what the strangers were packing, he said in a more somber tone, "I see you boys bringing back more than venison."

Kerlan came down from his horse and stood before the proprietor and the cowboys. "They're members of Gil Stuart's gang. We're taking them back to Deadwood."

The two cowboys stepped down from the porch to survey the bodies. Mr. Smith continued his conversation with Kerlan.

"We've all heard of the Stuart gang. It was 'bout time someone sent a few rounds their way. These boys here work at the Simons Ranch. They've had a few head taken from them by this bunch."

Kerlan turned to the two cowboys. "You work for Mr. Simons?"

"Yes, sir," the oldest of the two answered.

"I want you boys to ride back to the ranch and tell Mr. Simons that he can find his horses and cattle near a canyon a day's ride south of here. They're mixed in with animals from other ranchers. I've met your boss, and I know he's a fair man and that he'll try to get the livestock to their rightful owners. If he questions you, tell him Sam Kerlan told you this."

"We were on our way back to the ranch anyways," said one. "We'll give Mr. Simons your message."

Turning back to Mr. Smith, Kerlan said, "We'll take your offer of some food, and we'd also like to water and rest our horses awhile. We want to make Deadwood by tomorrow morning."

Catlin dismounted and took the horses to the water trough. After letting them drink for a few minutes, he took them over to the open corral, loosened up their cinches and removed their bridles, tying them off with ropes to the corral fence.

The mixed aromas of coffee, fried ham, and sweet jacks emanated from the cabin. Catlin washed his face in the horse trough and brushed the dirt from his clothes before going in to join Kerlan for breakfast.

***

As they gazed over a rise down into the misty little town of Deadwood, there was a disagreement in feelings between the two men. Kerlan saw a drafty little mining town whose inhabitants looked pale and ill. He preferred the sun and wind and open sky of the high plains, a place healthier for both man and beast.

But Catlin saw home. His warm room in the Drummond Hotel, a beef steak at Sadie's, a draught beer at the Number #10 and a visit to Suzie Wong. To Catlin, Deadwood was as solid as the rock cliffs above the town. This was his little harbor from the storm.

They moved down the steep path into the town. Stopping at the livery stable, Kerlan directed Catlin and the livery man to take the bodies over to the undertaker. He would notify the Sheriff. Drummond was coming out of his bank when he eyed the commotion at the stable. He saw Kerlan walking up the street toward him and went to meet him.

"Glad to see you back in one piece," said Drummond, obviously relieved and excited. "How'd it go? Is Catlin all right?"

"He's fine. We caught up with the gang a few days south of here. We got them in a crossfire and killed three of them. Stuart was wounded and got away with another man."

"Do you think he'll be back?" questioned Drummond anxiously.

"I'd have my doubts. Stuart knew that time was running out for him. He'd stayed too long, over worked the area. Bad luck to overstay your welcome. If he's not dead, be my guess he's gone from the Hills."

Drummond was somewhat uneasy with Kerlan's remarks, as trustworthy, but coming from a man much experienced in these matters he accepted them.

"Come to my office tonight after all the commotion has died down. We'll settle up then."

Kerlan nodded. Drummond hurried off to the undertakers as Kerlan proceeded across the street to the Sheriff's office.

***

Sheriff Seth Bullock sat at this desk scrutinizing the most recent wanted posters. He was a large man with a walrus mustache. People commented that his appearance resembled that of Wild Bill Hickok.

Entering the office, Kerlan announced himself with a tip of his hat. Sheriff Bullock looked up from the posters on his desk and said, "You must be Sam Kerlan. I've heard about you. Had you checked out for Mr. Drummond."

"Your reputation also precedes you," returned Kerlan. "It's not many who haven't heard the name of Sheriff Seth Bullock of Deadwood, Dakota Territory."

The Sheriff warmed immediately to this man. Any mention of his own status in the West awakened great interest in Bullock.

"What can I do for you, Mr. Kerlan?" the Sheriff asked.

"We have three bodies down at the undertakers. Lesser members of the Stuart gang."

"If I remember rightly," said Bullock, "Stuart rode with a big mean German and a murderous Mexican named Sanchez."

"The German is dead but Stuart and the Mexican got away. Stuart was wounded, but we couldn't gather how badly."

"Well, sir," exclaimed Sheriff Bullock, "you did the people of the Black Hills a great service. If Stuart is alive he'll go and ply his trade elsewhere. If he's dead may his bones rattle in hell."

With his forceful character and eloquent speech, Kerlan could see why this colorful Sheriff was widely known. But he suspected that his reputation might be based a bit more on bravado than gun smoke.

The Sheriff pulled on his hat, and the two men strolled over to Swenson's Furniture Store, where a crowd had already gathered to view the bodies. The three were laid out on planks leaning against a hitching post. In the grisly Western fashion they were stripped to their waists so that the public could examine their wounds. The two young men appeared all the more youthful alongside the huge and hairy German. The undertaker couldn't get the younger boy's eyes to close, and he looked like a choirboy searching the heavens with an innocent gaze.

The sight disturbed Kerlan, and he said to the Sheriff, "If you have any questions I'll be over cleaning up at the hotel."

Bullock sensed his unease, and said, "I don't like this kind of spectacle either, but I guess it's our way of saying, 'Go against the law and you'll end up like this'!"

Kerlan nodded in understanding and went over to the hotel. He ordered up a hot bath and sent the desk man down to the saloon to buy him a bottle of rye whiskey.

Settling into the hot water, he pulled the cork from the bottle and took a long, hard drink. He sat in the tub for a full hour, soaking away the dirt and dust, the chill, the stiffness, the pain and the sorrow.

***

Sadie bustled through her busy café pouring coffee for her customers. She stopped by Kerlan's table and asked if she could top off his mug.

"Yes, thank you, Ma'am," Kerlan said, leaning back from his meal of beefsteak, beans, baked potatoes and apple pie.

As he took a drink of coffee, he noticed Catlin coming through the door. Kerlan noted that he was in his best Sunday-go-to-meeting suit; and that his hair was slicked back with axle grease. Catlin surveyed the crowded room, recognizing Kerlan at the back. He walked up to him and said, "I see you're mostly done, Mr. Kerlan, but mind if I join you?"

"Sit down. I'd like to buy your meal."

"Well, thank you, Mr. Kerlan, but that's not necessary."

"No bother, sit. What'll you have?" Kerlan asked as he waived to the waitress. Sadie came over to the table.

"The usual, Jack?"

"Yes, Miss Sadie," answered Catlin, "with an extra helping of beans, if you would."

Sadie left the table and Kerlan looked over at Catlin. A strong odor of toilet water filled the air. It was apparent that Catlin was going out "spooning" tonight.

"Big night planned?" asked Kerlan with a knowing grin.

Catlin's face reddened and he looked down at the table.

"Yes, sir. I'm going to see my woman tonight."

"It's nothing to be ashamed of, Catlin. I wish I were so lucky."

Catlin smiled and nodded vigorously.

"We had quite a couple of days out there," said Kerlan, changing the subject. "I wish we would have brought Gil Stuart in, instead of those boys."

"Mr. Drummond wishes that too," said Catlin. "He's worried Stuart will stay in the Hills, or come back with another gang."

"I don't believe that will be the case. It'd be bad medicine for Stuart to stay around. I think he's well out of the area."

"What are your plans?" queried Catlin.

"I'll be moving out tomorrow. I got something I need to do, and then I'll probably head south. Never could stand the winters in these parts."

"The reason I asked, well, Mr. Drummond would like to have you stay on awhile. Sort of take care of any trouble, ya know, and well…"

"No, I don't think that will be possible this time. Hired guns can go from heroes to villains pretty fast out here. Ever hear of Bill Teague?"

"No, sir, can't say I have."

"Well, Teague worked for a cattleman's association in Wyoming. He was doing a good job when all of a sudden he was charged with shooting a young sheepherder. Hung him for it. I knew old Bill, and I don't believe he could have done that."

Catlin nodded his understanding as Sadie brought him a large platter of food. He dug in with relish, and Kerlan could see the conversation would be muted from there on. He tossed two dollars down on the table and said, "I have an appointment with Mr. Drummond. Maybe I'll see you in the morning."

"Yes, sir, Mr. Kerlan," Catlin said through a mouthful of beans, "and thanks for the meal."

Kerlan stepped out onto the wooden sidewalk in front of the café and the hard goods store. He stood for a moment to set fire to a cheroot. The resulting circle of light illuminated a figure leaning against a wall in the alleyway. Kerlan recognized Sheriff Bullock staring over at him.

"Evening, Sheriff," Kerlan said, seemingly unfazed by the Sheriff's sudden appearance.

"Good evening, Mr. Kerlan," the Sheriff said, not the least embarrassed. "I imagine you're wondering what the Sheriff of Deadwood is doing in a darkened alleyway. I do it now and again. It's interesting what people will do in the dark when they don't think anyone is watching. I've solved a few cases this way. Maybe even prevented a couple killings. At any rate, I hope I didn't startle you."

"No, sir," Kerlan said, suddenly gaining a new admiration for this unusual man. "I know a little about the power of the dark myself."

"Will you be staying with us for awhile longer?" the Sheriff asked, beginning to walk with Kerlan up the street.

"I plan to leave tomorrow."

"Don't feel like I'm hurrying your stay," continued the Sheriff. "I don't like to have guns in town, but I know the difference between a good man with a gun and a bad one."

"I just feel the need to get back out on the prairie. It's been awhile and the hills got me a little closed in."

"Sure, I understand," Bullock returned. "I used to feel that way myself. Now I look at these little hills as lumps in a big old wooly blanket, and I feel as snug as a raccoon under a stump."

The two men stopped outside Drummond's office and shook hands.

"I'll bid you goodnight, now, Mr. Kerlan, and the best of luck."

"Thank you, Sheriff," Kerlan returned, "and keep an eye on those dark places."

The Sheriff smiled and walked off into the crisp and silent night.

Chapter Eleven

Drummond raised his eyes from his work as Kerlan entered the office. He hurriedly closed his accounts book and stood up to greet his late-night visitor.

"Sit down, Mr. Kerlan. I'm pleased you could come by. Care for a little brandy? A cigar?"

"No thank you, Mr. Drummond. I just came by to tell you I'll be leaving in the morning."

"So soon? It was my hope you would stay around awhile. Sort of get comfortable with our little town."

"I've got a couple things I've been meaning to take care of. I believe it's time to move on."

"I just want you to know that I'll always have work for you here. I just wanted you to know that."

"Thank you. I'll keep it in mind."

"As for payment, I have it right here."

Drummond reached into the top drawer of his desk and withdrew a large envelope. He took from it a large stack of bills and began counting them out before Kerlan. At a certain amount Kerlan stopped him.

"That's all I'll take for now. Our original deal was to remove the Stuart gang from the Hills. You keep the remainder. If Stuart stays out of the Hills, you can send the money to an address in Cheyenne. If he doesn't, you let me know and I'll come back for him and the money. Call it a guarantee."

Drummond hesitated, but by Kerlan's tone and demeanor he knew he could agree to nothing else.

"Fine," agreed Drummond. "How will I be able to make contact with you?"

"I'll give you the name of a lawyer in Cheyenne. You can send him the money by stage if Stuart stays away."

Kerlan took out a piece of paper from his waistcoat and handed it to Drummond. Drummond read the name silently.

"Remember that name. He'll be Governor of Wyoming one day."

Drummond smiled and shook his head slowly.

"If that's all," Kerlan said standing to leave. "I'll say goodbye to you, Mr. Drummond. I'll be packing out at first light."

Drummond extended his hand and said, "I again want to thank you for your work. It isn't often I get a guarantee, and I appreciate that. I'm sure Stuart is out of the Hills, and I'll be sending you the remainder of the money soon."

"Take your time and be certain. Goodbye, Mr. Drummond."

"And goodbye to you, Mr. Kerlan."

***

After a restless night's sleep, Kerlan moved about his hotel room readying his gear for the journey ahead. His decision was made. He had not decided during the trip with Catlin, or during the last month, nor even six months ago. It was a decision he came to over time. One which was inevitable, that had stalked him for several years. It was a decision that had been waiting for him to make.

The night before he had told the livery to have his roan ready first thing in the morning. He carried his gear out of the hotel and walked the short distance to the stable. A stable boy was brushing his horse down, and it whinnied in recognition of its master. Kerlan rubbed the horse's neck and whispered to it. He turned to the stable boy and said, "I'm heading over for some coffee. Give him a good working over and saddle him up for me."

The stable boy nodded and continued with the brushing. Kerlan ran his hand several times from the horse's forehead to its nose. Then he strolled out of the stable and over to Sadie's eatery.

There was a fairly thin crowd at this time of the morning. A few miners and lumbermen were enjoying their morning repast and hardly looked up as Kerlan entered. He sat down and Sadie poured him a large mug of coffee. He ordered eggs and a side of ham before taking his first drink of the strong brew. Coffee was a morning necessity for Kerlan, and he carried it with him on the trail. He could go without breakfast of a morning, but without a wash of the bean brew he wasn't going to get his day off as he desired.

People came and went in the café while he finished his breakfast. He had a couple more cups of coffee, and readied a cheroot for fire. He sat back and blew blue smoke into the air. After a few more inhalations, he put money on the table and walked back to the livery.

The roan was saddled and ready. Kerlan tied his gear to the saddle. He checked his riggings for wear and tightened up the cinch. He led the horse over to the stable office and paid the man for the roan's keep. After leading the horse out into the street, he put his foot in the stirrup and pulled himself into the saddle. The roan shook its head and neck, and seemed to indicate to his master that he was ready to go. Kerlan reined the horse around and started down the street.

Drummond and Catlin were sitting in the assay office as Kerlan passed by.

"There goes Mr. Kerlan. I got to say goodbye to him," Catlin said excitedly.

"Let him be, Catlin," commanded Drummond. "I believe he said his goodbyes yesterday. But take a good last look at him. A man like Sam Kerlan won't be likely to pass through Deadwood again soon."

Catlin watched out the window as the gunman rode by. He thought of their time together on the cliff above that canyon of death. Although Catlin could not put his thoughts into words, he knew that when you shared danger with a man you created a special bond with him. Catlin's eyes focused. He would not soon forget Mr. Sam Kerlan.

Chapter Twelve

The logs on the fire burned quietly and cast a golden light on the otherwise darkened room. Shadows played against walls displaying the heads of deer and antelope and the massive head of a lone buffalo. Above the fireplace a Hawken fifty caliber rifle hung, its coat of dust indicating it was no longer its master's favorite. However, next to the fireplace leaned two Winchester rifles whose well oiled appearance revealed their frequent use and care.

Log fell against log in the fire and caused Ben Talbert to stir from his nap. He often fell asleep in his rocking chair these cool, fall evenings. Worn out with the work on the ranch and the raising of three children, he nodded off easily after the evening meal.

He took up his pipe from the table and filled it with tobacco. Settling back into his chair, he stared restfully into the fireplace. He loved this time in the evening. The children were in bed, and his wife moved quietly about finishing up the daily household chores. The time allowed him to make plans for the next day's work and to reflect on the work he'd completed that day.

His wife, Irma, knew intuitively how much this time meant to her husband and went out of her way to safeguard it for him. She had put the children to bed but was finding it difficult to get the older boy settled at the early evening hour. She promised him that she would talk with his father about his staying up a little later in the evening. The younger boy and girl complained as well but always fell asleep as soon as they lay their heads on the pillows.

The children were Irma's pride and joy. Far from becoming complacent through the daily routines of motherhood, her love for her children seemed rather to grow with each day. She sometimes cried at night thinking of the time when they would leave her.

Irma finished her duties and took the chair opposite Ben. He looked across at her and smiled warmly. She returned the affectionate gaze. Neither spoke; they seemed unwilling to break the peaceful silence. Irma took up her knitting and Ben refilled his pipe as each returned to their own thoughts.

In time Irma put aside her work, stood, and walked across to Ben. Leaning over she kissed him on his forehead and brushed his greying hair with her hand. He took her hand and stood up from the rocker. It had been a long day and they were both tired. They walked arm in arm into the younger children's room. Sammy was sound asleep with thumb in mouth and didn't stir when his mother kissed him. Laura was out of her covers, and her father gently tucked her in. Her blond hair lay shining about her head and her beauty gave her father pride. They left the room and quietly passed Benjy's room. They had stopped checking on him at night after the boy told them he was too big to be treated like a child. Although he was still their child, they respected his coming manhood by not bothering him with their nightly ritual. They entered their own room and silently closed the door behind them.

Outside the ranch house the fall air was chill and moist. An owl in a tall tree eyed a field mouse near the corral buildings. The owl flew from its perch and hovered for a moment in mid air. Folding its wings the owl made a dive for the tiny animal. The mouse seemed to sense the danger and quickly moved into a crack in the corral wall. The owl stood for a moment on the ground and then flew up to resume its vantage point in the craggy tree.

***

The Bad River Ranch was Ben's pride and joy. He built his dream through a combination of luck, foresight, and careful management. He traveled out from Minnesota with Roy McCrea, four horses, sixty head of cattle, some savings and a prayer. They held up that first winter in a sod house on the Bad River, almost going stir crazy waiting for spring to arrive. Luckily, it was a fairly open winter and the livestock were able to forage through the snow. Ben traveled to Ft. Pierre to buy supplies when the snow finally cleared. Upon returning he found Roy sitting forlornly outside the sod house. It seemed that a Sioux war party had passed along the Bad that morning and helped themselves to most of the cattle. Among those few head was the breeding bull they had brought out from Minnesota.

Ben, however, was a shrewd and careful businessman and had held some money back for such circumstances. He restocked his herd from a rancher on the Missouri who was selling out and moving south. He was even able to purchase two fine bulls to serve as the foundation of the herd's growth.

Ben was not the type of man to step mildly into the eye of a storm. He had made his plans years in advance of his move to Dakota Territory, saving every extra cent from his hardware store in Springfield. He studied, late into the night, the methods of raising cattle, bovine diseases, and anything else an aspiring cattleman would need to know.

The people of Springfield were surprised when they heard of his decision to move west. After all, he had an enterprising business, a nice home, a wife and a young son to care for. Why, they thought, should he risk all he had for some dream on the bleak Dakota prairie?

His wife hadn't questioned Ben about his plans. She loved him and was willing to go anywhere with him. His dream was hers because she couldn't think of life without Ben Talbert. Ben knew the first two years on the ranch would be the roughest. He decided Irma, now in her first few months of pregnancy, and Benjy would stay with relatives in St. Paul while he and Roy set out and worked to make the ranch a fit place for a family to live.

The Talbert's couldn't remember a time when Roy McCrea wasn't a part of their lives. He'd been the Springfield town drunk until Ben helped to sober him up by giving him a job in the hardware store and a place in his home and family. Ben and Roy worked long hours in the store and in the slow times would discuss their mutual dream of leaving narrow-minded Springfield for the freedom of ranch life. Although between them they couldn't discern the front from the back side of a cow, the vision of a new life of freedom on the prairie gave them incentive to learn. On Sundays they would ride out to a farm near the town. There they learned to rope a steer, pull a calving cow, and the many other tricks-of-the-trade which would be necessary for running a ranch. Through shared work and shared dreams, the two men came to know each other well. Ben was tight lipped about his personal affairs, but if any man knew his inner thoughts, it was Roy McCrea.

Ben and Roy did not waste any time those first couple of years on the ranch. During the first summer, while the cattle grazed lazily on the open prairie, they constructed two small corrals out of poles made from trees near the river. The poles were tied together with rawhide strips and bits of wire brought from Minnesota. At the open end of one corral, they built a large lean-to for calving and nursing sick cattle. This was constructed from lumber they had brought with them, as the trees along the river were quickly thinning out.

The next job was to build a solid ranch house since a sod house, though common in the area, would never do for Irma and the children. Ben had definite plans. He wanted four rooms: a large one for the kitchen, cold storage and sitting area, and three bedrooms, one for Irma and himself, one for the children, and one for Roy.

The money Ben had put away was dwindling fast, but he judged that they had enough to complete the house. He and Roy traveled to Fort Pierre and purchased the lumber along with some basic supplies. They worked as quickly as possible, as Dakota summers were oftentimes short. The ranch house was skirted in fieldstone and had a solid, wood floor. The walls and roof were sturdily built, for Roy had been a skilled carpenter before his drinking days began. The two men worked on the house steadily day and night for several weeks, while still finding time to mind the cattle and put in a large vegetable garden. When the house was finally completed, Ben broke out a bottle of Scotch whiskey he had been saving, and they drank a small toast to their future on the Bad River Ranch.

Chapter Thirteen

Ben lifted the saddle from the ground and gently placed it on Cyclone's back. The young gelding knew what was coming and playfully expanded its stomach. The horse tried this trick every once in awhile and it always caused Ben to smile to himself. He placed his knee in the horse's stomach and gently applied pressure.

"Com'on, Cy, quit foolin' round. We got a heap of work ahead of us today."

The horse gave in to its master and Ben tightened the cinch strap around its belly. The horse stood still while Ben mounted, but gave a playful leap once he was secure in the saddle. Ben loved this horse and although he'd ridden many in his time, Cyclone was his favorite.

Irma came out of the ranch house and stood on the porch. She breathed in the fresh morning air and looked toward the low hills, luminous in the new morning light. She watched her husband as he rode toward her.

"You going to be all right till tomorrow?" he asked her.

"I'll be fine. It's you I'm worried about. Why aren't you taking Roy with you? It seems like a two man job."

"I sent Roy into town to hire a couple hands. We have to gather up the herd and get them ready for the drive to Rosebud. Anyway, I'm just going to check the corral in the valley and do a head count."

Ben looked down from his horse onto his wife's face. "Woman," he said, "you worry too much. I can take care of myself."

Irma smiled and said gently, "Yes, I know, but, be careful. There are some tricky passes up in those hills."

"And Cyclone knows every one of them," Ben assured her.

The two of them looked at one another and knew enough had been said. Irma took a step forward and stood by the horse's side. Ben kissed his hand and held it to Irma's cheek. Irma stood back as Ben turned Cyclone and trotted out of the ranch yard.

Horse and rider paced along the river at a slow trot. Ben then moved Cyclone into an effortless canter. The horse seemed to be feeling its oats and wanted to open up on this cool, autumn morning. Ben gave him his head, and Cyclone broke into a freewheeling gallop. Ben pulled his hat tightly on his head and let the horse go for all it was worth. Both horse and rider enjoyed such runs. It did both body and soul good to let loose now and then.

They continued this pace for some time. Coming to a small stream branching off from the river, Ben guided Cyclone into a wide circular turn, slowing him down until they came to a full stop. Ben let Cyclone get his wind back as he looked up the stream. Several miles up this little band of water his cattle grazed on summer grass. In the next couple of days he would take a group of men up this stream to bring his cattle back to the ranch. There he would separate out the ones he intended to sell to the government. The holdovers would winter at the ranch.

Ben Talbert had a yearly contract with the government to supply cattle to the Rosebud Indian Reservation. Buffalo were a thing of the past and the reservation Indians needed a source of meat. Congress's law allotting each Indian 730 pounds of beef each year was a saving grace for Ben Talbert and the ranchers in the area because it assured them of a secure market for their cattle. The reservations were fairly close and there wasn't a lot of expense moving the cattle to them.

Beef issue day on the reservations was an amazing sight. Because the Lakota Sioux Indians were no longer able to go out and hunt for meat, they turned the day into a ritual hunt. Many wore ceremonial dress, and dances and other activities commenced. The Lakota's demanded the right to kill their beef. The result was a merciless slaughter with the Lakota's shooting down the cattle in closed corrals. Some even insisted on killing their quarry with bows and arrows while chasing them across open fields. Afterward they would enter the pens and claim their kill. They would skin and clean the beef in the old buffalo tradition, using every part of the animal. Government agents allowed this ritual as it seemed to appease the Indians and kept them from wandering off the reservation.

Ben let Cyclone take a short drink at the creek and then continued upstream several miles to where his cattle were grazing in an open expanse of prairie. The cows were not startled by his arrival since he was a regular visitor during the summer. Though peaceful now, the herd had to endure various dangers during the summer. Besides the four legged predators of nature, there were predators that stood upright on two legs. Raids by the Sioux were becoming less of a problem as more moved to the reservations. Rustlers, on the other hand, now posed a serious problem to ranchers in the area. As the beef trade became more stable and lucrative as a result of government contracts, rustlers had became bolder and more active. Ben himself had never lost any cattle, but he knew of other ranchers who had been rustled. At a meeting at a local ranch a fortnight ago there was even talk of bringing in a stock detective.

Ben didn't care much for the idea of vigilante justice but could understand the concerns of the other ranchers. He kept his own counsel for he knew how intensely some of his neighbors felt on the matter.

He and Cyclone worked the passes in the afternoon, looking for any stock which might have strayed. He found one yearling in a draw that had got its foot stuck in the bow of a fallen tree. He pried the foot loose and the calf ran down the draw in the direction of the herd, bawling for its mother.

He was glad to see there wasn't much death loss this past year. The grass and water had been good all summer, and the previous winter had been a mild one. The cattle were as strong as he'd ever seen them.

Riding back to the valley and through the cattle once more, Ben made his way to the campsite he and Roy McCrea had developed over the years. It was not fancy, just a few stumps surrounding a rock enclosure for cooking. The site sat up against a small rise that protected it from the wind. A couple of tall cottonwoods added to its security. Ben, Roy and Benjy had spent many hours here talking, dreaming and listening to the sounds of the prairie.

Ben removed the bedroll from his saddle and placed it by the circle of rocks. He took the saddle and bridle off Cyclone and tethered him on a long rope in the grassy field below the campsite. He started a fire and pulled out the fixin's Irma had prepared for him—a container of beef stew, some sourdough biscuits, two apples and a large slice of rhubarb pie all wrapped in a cloth. He warmed the stew and biscuits over the fire and sat down to an enjoyable meal. Although it may have been just his imagination, everything seemed to taste better out doors. He thoroughly savored the bounty of Irma's kitchen in the fresh air of a cool, prairie evening.

After the meal he lit up his pipe and leaned back on his saddle, listening to his cattle move about. Every now and then he would hear a mother baying for its young one. The stars in the sky were majestic in their brilliance, and Ben wished his son were present. Benjy took great pride in picking out the Big and Little Dippers, and pointing out the North Star to his father.

The red glow in the bowl of his pipe was growing weak and Ben tapped the remaining shads of tobacco into the fire. He stretched out upon his bed roll and continued looking up at the sky until the peaceful night overtook him and he fell into a restful slumber.

***

Irma was preparing beef and vegetable pie in the kitchen when she heard a commotion out in the ranch yard. She wiped her hands on her apron and went out onto the front porch just in time to watch Roy McCrea, Jed Cudmore and the McLaughlin boys ride into the yard. Jed had worked for her husband on occasion, but the McLaughlin boys were new to their employ. The boys had lost both their parents and younger sister in a fire the previous winter and had been hanging about Ft. Pierre doing odd jobs since the tragedy. Irma stood and waited while they rode up to her.

"Hello Boys," she said pleasantly.

"Howdy, Mrs. Talbert," answered the McLaughlin boys in unison.

Jed Cudmore nodded and Roy McCrea began, "Everyone's pretty much hired out of Ft. Pierre. Jed had some offers but held out for us. The boys here have been working at the livery and saloon. Said they would like a change of pace."

Irma nodded and said, "We're pleased to have them. Now you men go wash up and come in for supper. Ben should be back in the morning, and we better make sure you all get a good night's rest. There will be a lot of work to do."

Jed and the boys turned their horses toward the barn while Roy waited until they were out of ear shot.

"Slim pickens, Irma. I hope the boys can handle themselves. They seem to be good enough horsemen."

"I'm sure that between you and Ben they'll learn."

Irma hesitated for a moment and then continued. "Roy, I want to ask your opinion on something. Benjy has been pressing me to ask his father if he can come along on the drive. I don't feel good about it myself, but he wants it so bad. Do you think he's ready?"

Roy pondered quietly to himself. Young Benjy had been pestering him also about talking to his father.

"I guess I would say yes. We can keep a good eye on him, have him work the drags. I would say it would be better to break him in on this short trip than the longer one next year."

"Thanks, Roy," Irma said uneasily, grateful for the honest opinion yet still nervous about the prospect of her son out on the cattle drive.

Irma went back into the kitchen to lay out the meal and Roy turned toward the barn to get the boys set up for the evening. Jed took his usual place in the tack room, and the two boys set up their gear in the upper loft. A few years' earlier Roy and Ben had built an addition onto the barn so that Roy could have a place to himself. It was a large, airy room that served as a bedroom, sitting room, and kitchen. In the middle was a large pot bellied stove. Roy took most of his meals with the family, but thoroughly enjoyed the peace and quiet of having a place of his own.

As soon as the men had settled in and cleaned up, Roy led them over to the main house where Irma had set out a fine meal of beef pie, corn on the cob, and fresh baked choke cherry pie. The Mclaughlin boys were particularly enthusiastic about the fare, saying it reminded them of the meals their mother had cooked for them. The younger McLaughlin struck up a conversation with Benjy. His sense of excitement and his eagerness for adventure was contagious. Benjy's desire to accompany them was so intense that it almost made him physically ill.

After the meal the men gathered on the front porch. Roy and Jed discussed the upcoming drive as the older McLaughlin boy whittled. The two younger boys talked excitedly about horses and of seeing the Indian people on the reservation. The McLaughlin boy told Benjy about his uncle who had been with Custer at the Little Big Horn. The graphic description of what happened to the uncle sent shivers up and down Benjy's spine.

Irma put the two younger children to bed and came out on the porch to take in the cool evening air. The men acknowledged her respectfully and continued their pursuits. Irma looked to the low hills and thought of her husband. Ben always came back refreshed from his overnight stays. The open sky and the sounds, sights and smells of the prairie seemed to invigorate him.

Roy stirred her from her thoughts with his suggestion that the boys bed down. Tomorrow would be a busy day. He wanted the men up early to prepare the horses and tack and to pack for the journey. He figured Ben would be back by midmorning and would want the men ready by the following morning to bring the animals back to the yards.

The McLaughlins politely bid goodnight to Irma. Young McLaughlin and Benjy shook hands excitedly, as if they shared a secret.

Roy, Jed and the boys strolled off toward the barn. Irma quietly put her arm around Benjy's shoulder as they watched the men depart.

"Ma," Benjy interrupted the silence. "You will do what you can with Pa, won't you, Ma? I don't know what I'd do if I can't go on this drive."

Irma looked into the face of her son. He had grown so much taller in the last year that she hardly had to look down.

"Yes, Benjy. I'm on your side on this. I'll do what I can, but you must accept your father's decision on the matter without any back talk. He's your father and it will be up to him."

Young Benjy shook his head in dour affirmation, and the two of them entered the ranch house for the night.

Chapter Fourteen

By mid-morning everyone on the ranch had been at their tasks for several hours. Irma and Laura were in the kitchen preparing food while the men were readying horses and equipment. Roy and Sammy were in the tack room putting the finishing touches on some gear. Jed and the elder McLaughlin boy were trimming up horses hoofs while Benjy and young McLaughlin walked around the fences in the yard strengthening any boards that seemed wobbly and unable to hold in the large numbers of cattle that would soon be held there.

Into the midst of this furious activity rode Ben Talbert. He could see at a glance that Roy McCrea had supervised the preparations well. He was never concerned about leaving such tasks in Roy McCrea's hands. Roy worked as if the ranch was his own, and indeed, over the years Roy had been given a share of the proceeds from the sale of cattle and horses.

Roy came out of the tack room to greet Ben. Sammy ran to his father as he dismounted and grabbed onto one of his legs.

"Hi ya, Sammy boy. Did you miss your old pa?"

Sammy giggled as his father tossed him playfully into the air. Ben set him down and he ran off toward the house to tell his mother of his father's arrival.

"How'd you do in Ft. Pierre?" Ben asked Roy.

"It was a bit picked over, Ben," Roy replied. "Jed is back, of course, and I got the McLaughlin boys. They're young but willing, and I think they'll be fine."

Ben thought about the boys for a moment and replied, "Got to start sometime."

Roy looked at him knowingly. "Sure do."

Ben removed the saddle and bridle from Cyclone and turned him in with the rest of the horses. As he shut the gate, he said to Roy, "The cattle are looking real good. They're pretty well gathered, so we won't have much trouble bringing them in. Grass looks fine. Been a good year."

Roy smiled in agreement. The sense of satisfaction the two men felt about their work on the Bad River did not need to be expressed in words.

Ben heard his wife calling him from the porch, and he walked over to greet her as Roy went back to his duties in the tack room.

The work continued until late in the afternoon with Ben and Roy keeping a close eye on the preparations. Everyone was tired when they sat down at Irma's bountiful table to a meal of roast turkey with all the fixins. Everyone ate their fill while listening attentively to Ben as he instructed them in their individual tasks. He told them that once the cattle were gathered Roy would ride lead with Jed and himself at either flank. The McLaughlin boys would ride the drags. Ben warned them to move the cattle easy, to let the animals think they were making their own way. Driving cattle can be a subtle thing, Ben insisted—a man takes control while seemingly giving it away. He told the boys that they would soon get the feel of it.

Benjy's heart sank as he listened to his father. His father was ignoring him, and he felt it unfair. Billy McLaughlin was only two years older than he was, and Benjy felt that he had more experience around cattle and horses than both the McLaughlin boys put together. Irma watched her eldest son as her husband spoke and felt deeply the boy's sadness.

After the meal the men reposed on the front porch. Ben smoked his pipe while Roy and Jed rolled their own. They talked quietly in a haze of blue smoke while the boys pitched pennies against the steps.

After a time Ben tapped his pipe and excused himself. He went into the house where Irma was working on her sewing. He took the chair opposite her and began slowly.

"Dear, I did a little thinking out with the cattle last night. I know you won't like this, but I believe it's time Benjy comes along on one of these drives. I know you feel he's a little young, but he's a good horseman and beyond that he's interested in the cattle and the ranch and I want to encourage that interest. If you object I will back off, but these are my feelings on the matter."

Ben interpreted Irma's initial surprised expression to mean that she disagreed with his proposal. She looked down at her sewing for what to Ben seemed an eternity before saying, "If you feel he's ready, Ben, I won't object."

Ben breathed a sigh of relief and smiled broadly. He stood up and gave his wife a kiss on her forehead before walking back out on the porch.

The men and boys were sitting lazily about the porch when Ben came out amongst them.

"Boys," he said, "it's going to be a long day tomorrow, so I think we all better get some rest."

The group muttered agreement and moved off to their respective beds. Young Benjy said goodnight to Billy McLaughlin and turned to enter the house. Ben stood in front of his son and said, "Are your horse and tack ready for tomorrow?"

Benjy couldn't believe his ears. He could only stammer out in astonishment, "Paaa!"

He jumped forward and grabbed his father about his waist as he buried his face into his father's chest. The two held each other for some time. When they broke to look at one another, each had tears in his eyes.

"Thanks, Pa!" Benjy said at last.

"You go to bed now, Son. We have a big day ahead of us tomorrow."

Young Benjy leapt excitedly into the house as his father stood alone on the porch. Ben looked at the starry shroud over the low hills along the Bad River. The owl in the big cottonwood hooted a number of times. After a few moments, the light in Roy's room went out. Ben Talbert smiled to himself and entered the ranch house.

***

They were up before daybreak saddling horses and preparing for the drive. As the sun nudged over the horizon, the riders were in their saddles and moving out of the ranch yard. Irma watched from the front window. She saw Benjy proudly riding at the back of the group. The sight both pleased and worried her, but she knew the decision to let him go was the right one.

Ben Talbert led the group with Roy and Jed Cudmore at his side. The boys brought up the rear, full of anticipation at their first cattle drive.

They traveled down the Bad River for a time before taking the small fork to where the cattle were grazing. The presence of so many riders startled the cattle at first, so Ben instructed his drovers to ride among the cattle to get them comfortable with the horses and riders.

The men and boys separated and moved in and out of the herd. In time the cattle began to ignore the riders. Ben directed Jed and the McLaughlin boys to stay with the main herd while he, Roy and Benjy worked the passes for any strays. By his estimate most of the herd was intact, but there would always be a few who wandered away.

There were more cattle in the passes than Ben had figured. He and Benjy brought out singles, cows with calves at side, and small groups for Roy to hold until they could move them to the main herd. The single cows were nervous, but seemed to settle down when gathered together with the herd.

Ben and his son were moving up a small pass when they spotted two cows munching leisurely on high grass. At the sight of the two riders the cattle bolted up the side of a small hill. Benjy spurred his horse and rode to the crest of the hill, circled them back down the hill to the bottom of the pass and turned them in the direction of Roy and the small herd. The feat, executed so naturally, struck Ben Talbert with both amazement and pride.

They continued to work the passes for several hours until a sizeable number of cattle were gathered in the small meadow, and held by Roy. Ben decided they should move these cattle up the draw toward the main group. The cattle moved gingerly at first, but catching wind of the larger herd they began to move at a faster pace. Benjy seemed concerned with the sudden change until Roy rode beside him and assured him this was normal. The small grouping was simply anxious to rejoin the bulk of the herd.

The horsemen settled into quick canters behind the small bunch of cattle as it merged with the amassed herd. The cows bayed loudly and moved about excitedly. The cowboys watched warily until the animals settled down to grass and water.

Ben and Roy rode back to the passes after a quick meal and a cup of coffee. Benjy was directed to stay behind and assist Jed and the two McLaughlins. As Benjy and Billy rode the periphery of the herd, Benjy told him of his morning ride in the draws. Billy listened wide-eyed. Both boys were happily lost in a world of new and wonderful experiences.

Jed Cudmore reached back into his saddle bag and drew out his harmonica. The first few notes gathered the cattle's attention, but in a short time the melody seemed to lull them into a peaceful trance.

Ben and Roy kept at the passes until late in the afternoon. They gathered a few more head and concluded that most of them were accounted for. This drive had been far easier than the one two seasons ago when an early storm disoriented the cows and they were scattered all over creation. But this year the grass had been good, and this seemed to keep the cows together. This proximity also helped against predators such as wolves and coyotes.

They gathered their last bunch together and moved them toward the big herd. The same scenario took place and the pace quickened as they neared the larger grouping. The herd paid little attention as the few stragglers joined them. The new arrivals stomped and bellowed, and Ben imagined that this neglect hurt the smaller group's feelings. Ben then smiled, catching himself once again interpreting animal's actions in human terms.

Ben began to set out the vittles Irma had prepared, while directing the boys to feed and water the horses and prepare them for the night's watch; the horses would have to be unsaddled, brushed down and their hooves checked before being resaddled and tethered near the campsite. Two men would have to be on watch at all times throughout the night. They would work in shifts, one team waking the other for their tour of duty. The horses stood ready if a problem were to develop during the night.

Ben rode the entire circumference of bovines. The cattle seemed at ease, milling about eating grass and taking long drinks from the river. Everything had gone off smoothly, but somehow Ben had the feeling that this year's roundup had been too easy. He just hoped that the quiet would continue.

After supper the boys took the kettle and plates down to the river for washing. Ben directed Roy and Jed to take the first watch, and to wake him and Benjy for the next tour after a few hours. The two men rode out to the herd while Ben and the boys settled in by the fire. Jed's harmonica could be heard in the distance. The melody lured the boys into a restful sleep. Cattle moved by them in their dreams.

***

Ben's peaceful slumber was interrupted by some movement over by the horses. He looked up to see Jed dismounting and felt that the few hours of sleep had pasted by too quickly. He stood stiffly and stretched his tall frame. Walking over to where Benjy was sleeping, he gently shook the boy. Benjy mumbled in half consciousness until he heard his father's voice.

"Come on, Son, it's our turn."

The boy rose quickly and followed his father to the horses.

"They're real quiet," Jed informed them. "Roy is waiting with the herd till you come."

"Thanks, Jed," Ben returned. "You get some sleep. Benjy and I will take the rest of the night."

Father and son rode out to where Roy was waiting on a rise overlooking the herd. Ben told his son to ride to the other side of the herd and take his watch there.

"Be on the lookout for coyotes," he said as the boy rode away from him.

Ben took Cyclone up the rise and came abreast of his old friend. The two didn't talk for some time. Instead they just proudly watched the large herd they'd built together. In time Ben broke the silence.

"You'd better get some rest, Roy. They look pretty peaceful."

"Yeah," answered Roy. "I'll see you early." He prodded his horse down the rise and over to the encampment.

Ben reached inside his coat and pulled out his pipe and a pouch of smoking tobacco. He lit the pipe and took a soothing draw from the curved stem. He looked over the large herd and thought of his boyhood days on the Mississippi in Southeast Minnesota.

When Ben first read <u>Tom Sawyer</u> as a young married man, he had devoured the book. It reminded him of growing up in Red Wing, Minnesota, bringing back memories of the great paddle wheelers moving up and down the lazy river, and of the boyhood adventures he had with his brother and their friend Gilly.

Gilly was a colored boy whose mother cleaned house for Ben's parents. Gilly would come over with his Ma and he and the Talbert boys would go down to the river to fish or swim. The boys built their own raft, and on one occasion had gotten caught in a current and drifted all the way down river to Wabasha. They hitched a ride back on an empty grain barge heading to St. Paul. All three of them had their backsides tanned without mercy when they arrived safely home.

Ben missed Gilly. He was an open, friendly boy who was always eager for the next adventure. Gilly had drowned while swimming in that big river one mid-summer afternoon. The authorities dragged the river for days, but his body was never found. Ben remembered going with his father to tell Gilly's Ma. They sat with her for some time in the small shack outside Red Wing. Ben remembered, like it was yesterday, how she sat by the small stove in her rocking chair, tears streaming down her ample cheeks, repeating to herself, over and over, "Gilly's gone. My Gilly's gone."

Later, that night, Ben and his brother sat up in their room and cried until a restless sleep overcame them. In the middle of the night his brother awoke screaming. Ben climbed into his bed and held him until he stopped.

The river. Gilly. His brother. Good times, bad times. As time passed, things changed. Their father died at his desk in the bank where he worked as a loan officer. His brother went west to seek his fortune, while Ben and their mother went to live with relatives in Springfield. An uncle took him into the hardware store. Time passed…

A noise and the movement of cattle on the other side of the herd brought Ben back to the present. He took Cyclone down the rise and around the herd. Reaching the other side, he saw Benjy desperately trying to catch his horse. It was apparent the youngster had fallen asleep and dropped out of his saddle. Ben was amused by the sight, but as he came up to the boy he was careful to appear serious.

"What are you doing chasing around a saddled horse in the middle of the night? Do you want to stir up these cows?"

"Sorry, Pa," answered the boy sheepishly. "I guess I fell asleep."

Ben appreciated the boy's candor and said, "Get back on that horse and stay awake, and remember, it's a lot farther down to the ground than falling out of your bed."

Benjy smiled as he finally caught his horse. "Thanks, Pa, I'll stay awake from now on."

Chapter Fifteen

Daylight broke gently over the long, low hills by the river. Ben could smell bacon and coffee and knew Roy was already preparing a hearty breakfast that would help the men make it through the long day's work.

Ben could see his son on the other side of the herd. Benjy looked tired but vigilant, wary lest he repeat his previous night's lapse.

Ben started back to the camp and waved for his son to follow. The others were already eating when they arrived. Roy handed them each a platter as they dismounted their horses. They ate voraciously and washed the meal down with large cups of coffee.

The breakfast seemed to invigorate Ben, and he felt ready to take on the task ahead. He directed the youngest McLaughlin to clean up and ready the pack horse while the others mounted up. The elder McLaughlin and Benjy were to take up the drags. Jed and Roy were to ride either side of the herd. He would ride point and try to set a steady pace. Billy McLaughlin was to join the drags as soon as he was packed.

Each man and boy took up his station and waited for Ben Talbert to take the lead. Ben took off his hat and held it for a moment in the air. At this signal, the others began working the cattle, talking in low, solemn voices. At first the cattle were confused and resisted the horsemen, but as soon as those in the back started putting pressure on the ones ahead, they bellowed and began moving as a group. For a time the cattle bawled loudly, unaccustomed to having horses and men push them about. Many were searching for misplaced young ones.

Young Billy joined his brother and Benjy in the drags; the three of them kept steady pressure on the herd. Jed and Roy moved skillfully up and down the sides keeping renegade cows in place. The herd was moving fairly easily along, causing no great concern. Ben was careful to keep them at a certain set pace. This short trip back to the main ranch would be a good chance to instill in the cows a recognition that the men and horses were in charge. This would make the big drive to the reservation that much easier.

Even though they were eating a lot of dust, the boys in the drags were having the time of their lives. They had tied their bandannas behind their heads and pulled them up over their mouths and noses. Whenever a cow or calf would fall behind, one of the boys would gallop off and drive it back into the herd. At one point, the elder McLaughlin was driving a cow toward the rear of the cattle. The herd, startled by this action, surged ahead. Roy and Jed had to quickly ride ahead in a pincer movement and, with Ben's help, managed to hold them in place. Ben considered sending Roy back to the boys to tell them to be more careful, but decided the point had already been made.

They drove the cattle most of the morning, up the smaller stream to the Bad and then along the river to the flats a few miles from the ranch house. Irma and the young ones were waiting in a buckboard with a noon meal.

The men got off their horses and relaxed around the buckboard while eating their lunch. The boys were telling little Sammy about their adventures on the trail while the men planned the afternoon's work. They would have to cut the mature cows, mainly the steers and the cattle passed breeding, out of the herd and put them into the holding pens. These would be sold to the government. This would be difficult, as many of the cows still had calves at side and the weaning process was never easy. The calves would be the biggest concern, as the mother cows were well passed nursing and thus less attached to their young. Once the marketable cows were cut from the herd, the remainder would be driven to the pastures close to the ranch.

They mounted their horses and Ben began picking out the cows he wanted to sell to the government. Roy and Jed worked as a team, bringing them to the pen. Benjy kept any lonely calves from following. The McLaughlin boys worked the gate. In time everyone learned their role and the pen filled quickly. After a dusty, sweaty couple of hour's labor, Ben was satisfied with the number of confined cattle. Roy and the oldest McLaughlin were assigned to keep the penned cows quiet while Ben, Jed and the boys took the remaining cattle to the home pasture.

Before joining the others, Ben rode up to Roy with some final instructions. "Once we get the main herd home, I'll send Jed out to stay overnight with this bunch. If all goes well we'll be heading out tomorrow morning." Roy nodded, and Ben turned his horse and cantered off toward the moving herd.

***

Sitting before a large fire in the ranch house, Ben considered the task at hand. He puffed on his pipe, thinking through the final details of the drive ahead of them.

The previous two years they had driven the cattle north to the Standing Rock Reservation, but this year he had been told by Government Agents to take them south to Rosebud. It would be a shorter drive and the only river they would have to cross would be the Big White. According to Ben's calculations, the trip would take about five days, assuming everything went according to plan.

Roy and the older McLaughlin boy had rode up earlier that evening and reported that the cattle were doing well. Jed had spelled them and Roy thought that since the cattle had settled in well, Jed would have little work and be able to sleep most of the night. That was good news as Jed would be needed in the morning, and a fresh rider was always better than a tired one.

Ben believed that the drive should prove to be profitable since the government was paying top dollar. In addition to his own cattle, Ben had bought 250 heifers from a rancher east of the river. Ben had not discussed it with Irma, but he was also thinking of buying the Demsey ranch to the north. The Demsey's were poor managers, but had some of the best hay and grazing land in the area. Demsey had been one of the earliest settlers in that area, acquiring his land when he married an Indian woman. He wasn't the most ambitious of men and had indicated to Ben Talbert on several occasions that he might sell out for the right price. With Benjy coming of age and taking an interest in ranching it might be a good move to expand. If the government contracts continued for a few more years, and if other ranchers continued to look for replacement stock, expansion was very feasible. Ben's musings were interrupted when Irma came and sat in her chair opposite him.

"How long will you be gone, Ben?" Irma asked.

"I reckon five to six days down to Rosebud," her husband answered. "We should be back in half that time. I asked Phil Thorpe to drop in or send a man by every other day for you. If you have any trouble, be sure to let him know. The cattle are content on the long grass and there should be no problems."

"You look tired, dear, you should get some sleep."

Ben agreed with his wife and tapped out his pipe into the now smoldering fire. The day had been a long one, and once the drive began, it would be many days before Ben would be able to sleep in his own bed again.

***

Before the sun had warmed the horses' backs, saddles were up on them. Roy had shaken everyone in the barn out early and they prepared for the long journey in a steady and conscientious manner. After everything was ready, Irma had everyone in for one last home-cooked breakfast. The group ate quietly and hurriedly and soon was back out in the yard and up on their horses. Ben Talbert gave the little ones a hug and squeezed Irma's hand before mounting his own horse. Without further ado, they rode out of the ranchyard.

When they reached the pens, they found Jed, his horse saddled, ready for them. Ben directed the men and boys to spread out in a circular fashion before giving Jed the signal to open the gates. Jed accomplished this without dismounting, again impressing Ben and Roy with his horsemanship.

The cattle moved out of the pens in a steady surge. They gathered for a moment, unsure about what was happening to them. The cowboys, however, moved quickly and calmly to take control.

Ben moved to the point while Roy and Jed worked the drags for a time to move the cattle in behind Ben. Once the cattle were moving southwest, the boys took up the drags and the two experienced cowboys took their positions on either side of the herd.

It was a good start. The cattle seemed to catch on to the plan immediately and moved along in an easy manner. Their only resistance was expressed in a steady bellowing.

Benjy was in his glory. He moved back and forth behind the herd talking to the cows in low, soothing tones. Whenever a cow balked and stood stubbornly in place, he forced it back into the herd in a firm but unhurried way. The McLaughlin boys watched Benjy and learned from his example. Roy in turn, watched them all and judged that the youngsters all had the makin's to be fine cowboys.

Ben Talbert moved at the head of all this action breathing in the fresh air of a Dakota morning. Cyclone cantered enthusiastically under him. The horse's muscles rippled with excitement anytime he got close to a cow. Leading the large herd made the gelding almost prance in delight.

That same energy and excitement coursed through Ben Talbert's veins. It was for moments like this that he had left his staid life in Minnesota. Taking his herd to market was the annual high point of his life on the plains. For him, it was a moving feast.

Chapter Sixteen

All went as planned that first day out, and Ben was well pleased with the progress. At this rate, it might be possible to make Rosebud in four days.

The only unforeseen incident that day happened when the elder McLaughlin dismounted to relieve himself. He had put a rock on his horse's reins and walked behind a small hill for some privacy. When he was finished he found that his horse had rejoined the herd and left him behind. He had to run for a quarter of a mile but was able to catch up. A little embarrassment for the boy was the only negative result of the little drama.

It was early evening and Ben was watching for some good grass on which to settle the herd for the night. He cantered over to Roy and informed him that he would ride ahead to scout out a campsite.

A few miles from the herd Ben found a small valley full of high grass. The trouble would be water. Everyone would have to put in an extra long day tomorrow to get the cattle and horses to the Big White River for a sorely needed drink.

Ben dismounted and sat on a low bluff smoking his pipe and waiting for his herd. In time, a brown mass appeared on the horizon. Before long riders could be discerned.

Ben mounted and rode out to the herd. He again took up the point and led them to the grassy vale. The cattle began feeding on the grass and the riders circled to keep them in their place. In a short while the cattle had settled in, and Roy and Ben dismounted to set up the camp for the night.

Ben undid the pack horses, while Roy started a fire to heat the stew. Over the years he and Irma had developed an efficient system for feeding the men. She would prepare the fixin's for the number of days out on the trail, wrapping them individually in cloth. She prepared only the breakfast and evening meals, since the men were saddled up and working they would seldom stop for a mid-day repast.

Breakfasts were usually smoked and heavily salted bacon, hard buns and coffee. Evening meals consisted of a stew with dried meat, carrots and onions cooked together in a broth of spices. Irma packed fruit when it was in season and would include jars of her homemade jams for the men's sweet tooth's.

The cattle were distracted enough by the rich grass that Ben felt comfortable calling all of the men into supper. They sat around the fire and thoroughly enjoyed the flavor of Roy's stew. They washed it down with cups of coffee and each finished off with a large green apple that Irma had packed for them.

Ben decided he and Roy would take the first watch. He told the boys to settle down and get some sleep after they had cleaned up after the meal. The youngsters gathered up the plates and took them over to a sandy hill for a dry wash. The sand scrubbed away the particles of food, so only a small amount of water was required for the final rinsing.

Ben and Roy mounted their horses and rode out to the herd. Jed started a melancholy tune on his harmonica; the elder Mclaughlin rolled out his bedroll and was asleep as soon as his head hit the ground.

Ben and Billy sat by the fire listening to Jed's harmonica and to the other sounds of the prairie. Cattle bellowed in the background as Benjy laid back and watched the northeastern sky.

He saw a falling star and made a quick wish. A moment later, he saw another and then another, and sat up to see if his eyes were playing tricks on him. One after the other, they became bright and died out again; a continual progression of falling stars.

"Billy," he murmured to his young saddle mate. "Look up there yonder. Stars are falling all over the dern place."

Billy gazed up into the sky at the spectacle before him. He sat up, mouth wide open in astonishment.

"What is it, Benjy?" he asked in a startled tone. "Is it the end of the world?"

Jed Cudmore was also watching the luminous sky and was amused by the boys' reaction.

"Don't worry boys, it ain't Armageddon," he said with a wry smile.

"What is it, Jed?" the boys asked in unison.

"It's a night of falling stars, that's all. I've seen it a few times. An old cowboy once told me that your trail will be straight and true after a night of falling stars. A sign that good things are going to happen to you."

The boys watched enthralled for an hour or so. At first, Benjy tried to make a wish after each star fell, but as he couldn't keep up with them, he decided to make one general wish instead.

Ben Talbert and Roy McCrea were also watching the sky that evening. It struck Ben as a good omen for the first day of their drive.

***

Toward morning the cattle were moving about and lowing uneasily. Ben knew the cows were in need of water and decided to move them out at first light. The cattle's thirst would quicken their pace and the boys would have to be at their best to keep them under control. At the same time, Ben knew that the cattle were not totally dehydrated, for they had taken in some moisture from the high grass the previous night.

Roy rustled up Jed and the boys. They broke camp quickly and got up into their saddles.

Ben decided to move the herd in a close formation with Roy, Jed, and himself maintaining tight control of the point. The boys were told not to press the drags but rather to keep the cattle as peaceful as possible and to move at a slow, steady pace.

With such an early start, Ben calculated, the herd should make the Big White by mid to late afternoon. The cattle moved swiftly and bellowed loudly but the cowboys' maintained steadfast control.

The boys were still groggy from their early wakening, but even so could easily maintain the lethargic pace ordered by Ben. In his dreamy state, Benjy recalled the night of falling stars and speculated on what other wonders he might witness on his first drive.

The point was maintained expertly by the three experienced riders. Ben slowed the lead cows, while Roy and Jed moved up and down the front of the herd in fluid motions. Roy had come a long way since his clerking days in Springfield; he sat a horse as good as any cowboy and better than most.

On one of his swings up and down the face of the herd, Roy came alongside Ben's horse.

"They seem to be holding o.k.," he observed.

"They're fine now, Roy, but we've got to watch them close when we near the Big White. I'm fearful once they get the smell of water they might bolt for it and we might end up with some dead cows, not to mention men and horses."

"What's our plan then?" Roy asked anxiously.

"I believe we'll move everyone up to the front," Ben answered calmly. "There shouldn't be any need for riders on the drags since the cattle's only care will be water at that point. We'll try to hold them tight and hope for the best."

Roy nodded his agreement, turned his horse, and moved back to his duties. His trust in Ben's judgment was unquestioned.

The herd continued forward at a steady pace. Ben kept himself at the ready, knowing that once the cattle got wind of water, their disposition was bound to change.

The boys at the drags had finally shaken off the early morning doldrums and were focusing on their work. Benjy gently worked the cows, every now and then giving Billy the signal to slow things down. While Billy was enthusiastically taking to this new line of work, his older brother had already decided this would be his first and last cattle drive. After the drive was over, he would be more than ready to go back to working in a saloon or a store.

Ben felt a change in the mood of the lead cows. They were either thirstier than before or were beginning to sense that there was water ahead. He signaled Roy to ride up beside him.

"Go tell Benjy and Billy to join us at the front. Leave the other boy at the back but tell him not to put any pressure on the herd. I just want the cows to feel that there's somebody behind them."

Roy nodded and swiftly went about the task. Soon the boys joined the men at the front. Watching Roy and Jed, they quickly learned their new duties.

The pace quickened markedly as the boys arrived. The cows were now at a fast walk, while the cowboy's horses were set in a slow canter, moving back and forth at the head of the herd. Earlier on Ben had picked out the lead cow. She seemed to set the pace for the herd, and so Ben kept Cyclone's rump in this cow's face to slow her down. When the cow had gotten feisty a few times Cyclone would kick back at her temporarily diminishing her ardor.

Soon the horses also sensed the water and began to become restless. The cows had now worked up to a slow trot. The cowboys were working furiously, yelling and waiving hats and quirts to slow them down. This pace, kept up over several miles, was taking a toll on both the horses and the riders. Ben knew they must control the cattle as long as possible as the terrain was unsuited for a full out run. A number of cows would be killed if they broke free of the men.

The horses and men worked feverishly to keep control of the now bellowing and determined herd. The cattle were just short of a full out run and their pace was quickening by the minute.

Ben worked Cyclone at the point of the herd, moving him back and forth to hem in the lead cows. The other cowboys were now in full lope, riding from one side to the other, striving to keep the cows at bay.

Glancing up from his harried labors, Ben saw a blue band lying complacently on the distant prairie. Ben knew that the men need only maintain control for a few more miles. Roy and Jed had also noticed their destination, but the boys were too intent on their labors to see the watery ribbon on the horizon.

The cattle's nostrils were filled with the promise of liquid succor, and they finally broke out at a run. The position of the men and horses was precarious as one wrong move could bring down horse and rider under pounding hooves. Ben's first instinct was the safety of the boys. He moved Cyclone out front and steadily to one side until he came abreast of Benjy's pony, moving him off to the side of the herd. He then spurred Cyclone on to the other side and forced Billy's horse to safety. After assuring the boy's well-being, he galloped back to point where Roy and Jed were maintaining tenuous control.

The three riders set low in their saddles and rode hell's fury down to within a half mile of the river when Ben suddenly gave the signal to abandon the front of the herd.

Fortunately for both the riders and the herd, the land stretching to the river was flat and sloping, lacking the breaks so prevalent on the Missouri.

The lead cattle plunged into the small stream while the others spread out along the bank. After drinking their fill many just stood in the water to cool off.

The cowboys allowed their horses to drink sparingly, knowing it was unsafe to let an overheated animal drink at will. Ben glanced over at Roy and shook his head in relief. Looking back at the slope he could see the carcasses of several cows, trampled in the last mad rush to water. Rather than feeling regret, however, Ben was simply grateful that no bodies of horse or rider lay beside the dead cattle.

***

Making the best of the situation, Roy and Jed dragged one of the dead animals to a stand of trees near the river where they gutted and dressed it out, cutting off a rump roast and some steaks for the journey.

Ben and the boys kept watch over the herd. The cattle were complacently mulling about the rich grass near the river, content now that their thirsts were satisfied. Ben saw no trouble ahead for the evening and was glad of it; everyone needed a rest.

Roy began cooking a roast over an open fire. Jed played an Irish aire on his harmonica and the boys caught a few winks on their saddle blankets.

Ben rode up and down the creek looking over the herd. They were still largely intact after the long run to water. Their grazing now would put on any weight they might have lost in the riotous rush to the Big White. Except for the few lost head, the herd had fared well.

Ben planned to cross the cows over a few miles from where the Little White joined the Big White, and then move them down to Rosebud on the east side of the Little White. There would be no more trouble with lack of water. In a couple of days they would be near enough to let the cattle graze for a day before running them into the pens.

The smell of roasted beef filled the air and Ben edged Cyclone out of the cows and back to the camp. After dismounting, he loosened the cinch on his saddle, pulled off the bridle and tethered his horse nearby. Cyclone shook himself, whinnied, and began chomping grass.

Everyone was tired but hungry. Roy cut off large slices of roast and filled each plate with a heaping pile of fried potatoes. Each ate his fill, the young ones even going back for a second helping. After the meal, Roy dispensed coffee to the men and rock candy and apples to the boys. Ben sat back with his pipe and looked over some maps as the rest of the outfit relaxed around the campfire.

Roy could see that the boys were tuckered out so he took it upon himself to clean up after the meal. Afterward, he sat beside Ben and poured himself a cup of coffee.

"We were lucky today, Roy," Ben said after some time had passed.

"I believe so, Ben. If one horse would have missed a stride we'd be mourning over a grave right now."

"I'm going to let the boys and you rest tonight. Jed and I will take turns with the herd. We shouldn't have any trouble. The cows seem content."

The men sat silently for a moment. Roy gazed over at the napping Benjy and smiled to himself. Benjy was like a son to Roy and in many ways was closer to Roy than he was to his own father. Benjy could tell Roy things he would never tell Ben. The two had a bond that at times aroused Ben's jealousy.

"Benjy did you proud today, Ben. You ought to tell him how good he's done."

Ben pondered the comment for a brief moment and shook his head. "He knows he's doing right when I'm not telling him he's doing wrong."

"Yea," answered Roy. "But a boy needs to hear some encouragement from his Pa. Believe me when I tell you that," Roy said with a sudden hint of anger in his voice, "for I didn't get any from mine."

With that, Roy stood up and walked down to the stream. Ben watched him go, bewildered at the sudden emotion in his normally docile friend. But he simply put it down to the excitement of the day and took a long draw on his pipe.

Chapter Seventeen

The next day's movement was uneventful compared to the previous day's ride. The cattle ambled in a meandering fashion down the Big White; the drovers on either side gently prodding them toward their destination.

Ben rode at an easy pace, felling relaxed. Yesterday's dash to the river could easily have ended in disaster. One of the boys or men could have been killed, horses injured or more cattle lost. The loss of a few cows had been a small price to pay. Ben's thoughts now turned to the future. After two more long days they would be within a half day of Rosebud. There they would gather the cattle to let them feed and replenish themselves before driving them into the pens.

Ben would see an immediate reward for his labors. One of the advantages of selling cattle to the government was that agents would immediately issue a check for the price of the cows. This and last year's payment were pure profit for Ben and were earmarked for his planned expansion. Ben could see no limit to the future on the Dakota prairie. Between the reservation and the sale of cattle to new markets, both east and west of the river, Ben foresaw a steady demand for his herd.

With the help of Roy and the boys, particularly with Benjy now coming of age, Ben could gradually cut a cattle empire from the barren prairie.

Besides cattle, Ben had started to build up and breed out a remuda of horseflesh. He felt this would be a hedge against the possibility of a future weak cattle market. The horses were a combination of the thoroughbreds and Morgans of the east and the shorter, stouter Indian ponies of the west. After several generations of breeding, Ben had developed a strong, stocky cow horse. The horse was agile and quick in short bursts, important for controlling the unpredictable cows of the prairie. The horse had great stamina and with minimal training would cut and control cattle as if were born for the work.

Ben's own horse was a natural at this task. When cutting cattle from the herd, Ben rode to the bunched cows and loosened the reins about the horse's neck. The horse would lower his head, nose almost touching the ground, and in quick, speedy movements would cut and control the cows. The horse was a true American breed, blending the style and grace of the Morgan and thoroughbred with the feistiness and agility of the Indian pony.

The horse portion of his business hadn't been expanding like the cattle, but Ben was beginning to get some indications from the region that some good horse flesh would be welcome.

There would always be a market for good cattle horses and Ben believed that he and his ranch could fill that need.

Watching Jed Cudmore calmly and efficiently work the right flank of the herd furthered Ben's conviction that he would offer Jed a full-time job. The work around the ranch was getting too much for Roy and himself to handle alone. With Benjy able to take on some responsibilities, and the addition of Jed and possibly young McLaughlin, Ben would have the manpower to expand upon his dream. Ben had noticed how well the young McLaughlin lad got on with Benjy; his son needed a friend near his own age.

Young Benjy's voice cut into his father's musings. "How far do you think it is yet, Pa?"

"I believe we'll be on the outskirts of Rosebud in two days' time, Son. We'll hole up there for awhile to give the cattle some time to rest and then bring them into market."

"What's it like at Rosebud?"

"Well, Son, the government brought most of the Indians together there after Custer was killed. The people live in small buildings and teepees. Some farming and gardening are done on the outskirts of town. There's a church and a school where the youngsters are taught. The agent runs the town, and the Indian police see to it that nothing' gets out of hand. In a way it all seems a little unnatural. These people were hunters and warriors and wandered the prairie after the buffalo and provided for themselves. Now they put them in long pants and make them go to school. I don't rightly feel it's good for the Indians."

Benjy pondered what his father had said and asked, "Pa, what was it like in the early days when the Indians were still free? Were you afraid of them?"

"We were never molested ourselves, but there were some frightening incidents when we first got out here. A ranch family over on Medicine Creek was wiped out and some terrible stories were told about what happened to them. In those days, Roy and I would take turns night hawking. We always carried rifles with us, even around the barns."

"One day we were riding along Frozen Man Creek and came face to face with seven or eight braves on the other side of the water. They stared at us for awhile as we stared back. Roy and I were sure we were about to meet our maker when all of a sudden the lead brave raised his hand in salute, turned and rode off. The braves were out for fresh meat just as we were."

Father and son rode on together in silence. Benjy pondered the excitement of the early days, picturing all that his Pa and Roy had gone through. He wished, deep in his soul, that he could have been there with them. It seemed so exciting and dangerous.

Ben Sr. was thinking too—about what Roy had said to him yesterday after the hard ride to the river.

He cleared his throat and spoke hesitantly. "Son, uh, I just want to tell you… I am proud of how you handled yourself yesterday. I think you did a real good job and I… I…just mean to tell you I'm proud of you and glad to have you along."

"Thanks, Pa," Benjy said unaffectedly. "It was one heck of a day."

"Yes, Son, there's no doubt about that." His son's natural, matter-of-fact reaction put Ben at ease. "It was one heck of a day."

***

The Bad River outfit set up camp near a stand of cottonwoods on the Little White. The day had moved along easily and without incident, a welcome reprieve from the previous day's excitement.

Roy prepared a meal while the boys saw to the horses. After checking on the herd, Ben and Jed returned to camp, giving their horses to young McLaughlin.

Everyone settled in for a meal of beefsteak and fixin's and afterward relaxed by the fire. Ben, Roy and Jed discussed the cattle and the boys played a game of knife throw.

"Riders coming," Billy McLaughlin suddenly shouted.

The men stood up and looked out onto the prairie. Two riders were moving toward them at a fast trot, coming from the southeast. They looked like drovers, their long coats flapping in the wind.

"Strange to see men out in these parts," Roy commented.

"They must be part of a larger outfit," said Ben. "They're probably just out scouting some water. Put some fresh coffee on and throw a couple of steaks on the fire. They may be hungry."

The riders stopped a short distance from camp and one of the men took off his hat and waved to the people around the fire.

Roy in turn took off his hat and waved back in welcome.

The riders proceeded into the camp and stopped their horses before the group of men and boys.

"Howdy, folks," a tall, lean older man greeted them.

"Good day to you," returned Ben. "What are you fellas doing out and about in these parts?"

"We're driving up some horses from Nebraska. We heard the army might be interested in buying some horseflesh."

"I see," Ben returned. "You men hungry?"

"I reckon we could use some vittles. We were out for water and been gone from the remuda more than half a day."

"Well, there's plenty of water here along the Little White and north of here on the Big. You men dismount now and have yourselves a meal. These boys will take care of your horses."

"Many thanks," came back the tall horseman's reply. He and his partner, a drover in his mid-twenties, got off their mounts and gave the reins to Benjy and Billy. The boys led the horses to where the remuda was tied off and the drovers joined the men by the fire.

Roy prepared two plates brimming with steak, potatoes and hard bread. He poured the men two large cups of coffee.

The men were pleased with the fare for they hadn't had nourishment since an early breakfast.

"Where you boys heading with the cattle?" The tall man asked between mouthfuls.

"We're taking them down to Rosebud for beef issue day," Ben answered.

"I see. I heard you boys in this territory have a pretty regular market up here."

"Yea, it's been good for all of us," Ben said.

"Where you all from?" the tall drover asked.

"Up near Ft. Pierre on the Bad River."

The tall drover and his companion rolled cigarettes while Ben filled and lit his pipe.

After setting fire to his smoke the older man asked, "Do you know if there is any need for horseflesh in these parts?"

"That would depend on the quality and the quantity," Ben came back.

"We have about seventy-five head of good horseflesh, some with colts at side. Most of them came out of west Texas. Good cow ponies. We picked up twenty-five to thirty slicks along the way. Some of them ain't bad."

"Well," Ben said, "I'm always looking for good horseflesh. I don't know about the slicks 'cause we can pick those up ourselves. You say you're about a day's ride away?"

The tall drover nodded.

"Tell you what. We've got about two days drive into Rosebud. You're a day to the southeast and are probably within a day or so of Rosebud yourselves. If you want to bring your stock into Rosebud and if they're as decent as you say they are I'll make you a fair offer for them."

"Sounds like we may have a deal. I think you will be pleased with them. Some of the finest horseflesh north of the Platte."

"The slicks," Ben asked. "They aren't branded are they?"

"No, sir," the horseman returned.

"Good. This is open range and people are particular about branded stock. If there are no marks they're free pickens in my book."

"You boys settle in with us tonight," Ben continued, "and head out in the morning. We'll talk price in Rosebud after I've seen your string."

"You seem like a fair man," the horseman answered. "I believe we can come to an agreement. The name's Severson and I have a feeling we're going to make a deal."

***

The horses were saddled and the men up in them as daylight broke on the banks of the Little White River.

Severson and his man discussed the meeting arrangements with Ben and then rode into the new dawn's light.

Ben made a circular ride of the herd and checked with each man and boy, giving them individual instructions for the day's ride. He made a point to do this regularly because it showed each one of them that Ben took an interest in them and valued their opinions.

After seeing that all was well and getting a feel for the mood of the cattle, Ben waved his hat for the drive to continue down the Little White.

Benjy and Billy were again at the drags and moved back and forth, visiting for a few moments as they crossed paths. The older McLaughlin lad rode in a melancholy fashion. He did not bother to fan out but rode instead in a straight line at the back of the herd. The boy had decided after the first day that driving cattle was not his lot and thought only about the day when he would get back to people and civilization. Ben noticed the boy's lack of dedication but did not hold it against the youngster. Not everyone was born to the life.

Cyclone pranced happily at the head of the herd. This horse did not offer the most relaxing ride, as it was always in motion, ready in an instant to head off a belligerent cow or dash off into the leather-burning runs both steed and master so enjoyed. Yet Ben appreciated Cyclone's vigilance as it kept him on his guard. Many times the horse's wariness had helped Ben out of a crisis situation.

Ben loped across the face of the herd and came to a walk alongside Roy.

"How are the boys doing?" Ben queried.

"Real good," answered Roy. "That Billy McLaughlin has the makin's of a fine cowman."

"How do you think the cows are holding up?"

"They're losing a little weight," Roy observed. "But that's water loss. They seem to pick it up grazing at night."

The two rode on in silence for a time, enjoying the fine autumn day. They watched proudly as Benjy and Billy moved three delinquent cows back into the herd. Meanwhile Jed worked the right point, moving up and down the herd, keeping tight control.

Ben filled and lit his pipe, not an easy feat astride the active back of Cyclone. He turned to Roy and suddenly asked, "Ever think much about Minnesota?"

"Once in awhile," Roy answered hesitantly, taken aback at the unexpected question. "Sometimes I just miss the green. But I wouldn't trade it for what we got here."

"I was thinking," Ben continued. "Maybe we'll take a trip back someday. Irma's been yearning to see her relations in St. Paul, and it would be interesting to see how Springfield has fared since we've been gone. In a couple of years Benjy should be able to watch the place and we'll take some time off and head over."

"I think I'd like that, Ben," Roy said with satisfaction.

The cattle moved in and out of the river at will, the proximity to the elixir seeming to content them. Water was the lifeblood of the west river territory. Rainfall was minimal, but in a good year there was enough to nurture the high prairie grass and fill the streams and water holes. Though hard snowfalls and sudden winter storms presented some of the greatest perils to ranch life, the moisture derived from these winter blasts filled the rivers and streams, and these were the very veins of life to the range.

Jed spotted a small band of wolves across the stream and quickly gave chase. The wolves yelped and ran like hounds with their tails on fire. Jed pulled up his horse and chuckled to himself as the pack disappeared over a distant hill.

Ben and Roy watched Jed's ride with amusement. Wolves were a constant threat to a herd of cattle but generally stayed away when their instincts told them that men were about.

The wolves were in full stride and ran up and down several hills before looking back warily. Finally they gathered together on a low rise and howled at full pitch, partly in gratitude for having escaped their pursuer, and partly in anger at having been chased out of their own domain.

Chapter Eighteen

On the last, long day's ride to Rosebud the youngsters were full of anticipation. In his lifetime Benjy had seen a few Indians. Most of these worked as cowboys for outfits along the Missouri and dressed much like the other cowboys. Their unremarkable appearance had been a severe disappointment to the impressionable young man.

Benjy longed to see the Indians on their own ground, to examine a teepee, to see how the Indians really lived. His mind was full of his father's stories about young men dressing up in war paint, preparing to confront an enemy or to hunt buffalo for their families.

The fact that there were actual Indians out in the rangeland of Dakota Territory added a dimension of excitement to Benjy's life. He had been a youngster when Custer was cut down at the Little Big Horn, and later had seen the horse cavalry heading up the Missouri to Ft. Abraham Lincoln. He had wished he could have ridden with them.

As they began to encounter small settlements along the Little White, the older men knew they were nearing Rosebud. Most of the settlements were humble affairs of one or two homes made from cottonwood trees with roofs covered with sod. Some had a small corral. By others, a teepee stood, inhabited by older folks who could not get used to living in a house made of trees.

Benjy's jaw dropped in wonderment when he came across his first teepee. An old man and two small children sat before it, waving as the herd and drovers passed by. Benjy waved back in pure friendliness and excitement.

Ben kept the herd and his men moving at a steady pace in order to get to the outskirts of the village by nightfall. The pace did not seem to put any stress on the cows, but the riders were tired and looking forward to a rest and the sights and sounds of beef issue day. Although both Roy and Jed had experienced it before, they still felt a keen interest in the activities at Rosebud.

Ben decided to ride ahead and scout out grazing terrain outside the village. Signaling his intentions, he loped on ahead of the herd.

He had ridden along the river for two hours or more, enjoying the quiet when Cyclone suddenly snorted and stopped in his tracks, causing Ben to lurch forward.

"What's the matter, Cy?" Ben said, startled, and pushing himself back into his saddle. Cyclone snorted again, raised his front hooves, and pounded the ground several times.

Ben looked out on the horizon and saw what Cyclone had only sensed. A group of riders, ten or more, were heading toward them on the river.

As the riders drew closer, Ben suddenly relaxed. He recognized the riders as DuMarce and his bunch from up on the Cheyenne River. DuMarce had been one of the first cattlemen west of the Missouri River. He had married a Sioux woman and had a passel of children—Ben surmised that about half the riders were DuMarce's own sons.

Ben had ridden with DuMarce on a few of the big roundups. West River was open range, and in the early days cattle from various herds mixed together freely. Once every few years all of the big outfits, and some of the smaller ranchers, would go out on one big roundup to help everyone get their stock back. While a few were beginning to keep their cows on their own home range with barbed wire, most ranchers still followed the open range formula.

As Ben neared the riders, DuMarce also recognized his old friend. He took off his wide brimmed hat and waved in greeting.

"Monsieur Ben Talbert," he called when within ear shot, "greetings of the day to you."

"Good day to you, DuMarce," Ben answered in a friendly tone.

When the riders met, Ben could pick out DuMarce's sons. One could see both the French and Sioux blood in their strong and handsome features.

"So I see you too are driving a herd to Rosebud," said DuMarce.

"Yes," Ben returned, "and wouldn't you know that my shrewd French friend would beat me to it."

"The price is the same," DuMarce returned happily, "and your timing couldn't be better as they are butchering tomorrow. We would have stayed, but I must get back to my ranch as I have a bunch of horses that must be moved up north. I envy you tomorrow's enjoyment."

"I wish you could be there with us."

"Well Monsieur Ben, we both have work to do, I will let your men know your location. There is a good spot above the village to graze and water your cows. I will bid you adieu and invite you to stop by my ranch when you are up my way. Adieu, my friend."

"Good bye to you, my friend," Ben said as DuMarce and his riders moved north along the creek.

Ben continued along the river for some time before coming to the spot DuMarce had told him about. He dismounted Cyclone and loosened the cinch about the horse's belly. He took his pipe from his vest, packed it full, and waited for the arrival of his herd.

***

The sun was in its final arch toward the western horizon when Ben finally spotted the herd. He breathed a sigh of relief and rode Cyclone out to meet them.

Roy and Jed were at the front of the cows when Ben rode up to them.

"Good to see you boys," Ben said. "Did you run into the DuMarce outfit?"

"Yeah," Roy answered. "Seems like Monsieur DuMarce breeds his own cowboys."

Ben laughed and said, "I guess old DuMarce started from scratch with cattle and horses and used the same approach when it came to hands."

The two men chuckled to themselves until Roy broke the merriment. "Did you find a place for tonight?"

"Yeah, good grass and water right above the village. Just around those hills."

The men spread out and led the herd to the location DuMarce had suggested.

The youngsters were elated about being within walking distance of Rosebud. Along the way, they had encountered Indian families in small, Government Issue wagons heading in to get their beef. There was a festive air, since their journey was not just for business but for socializing as well. The Indians would see their many relations, do some trading, and buy some luxuries such as sugar, tobacco and hard candy for the children.

The herd reached the grass land and settled in by two water holes. The cows drank their fill and then munched contentedly on the high grass. The men moved about them on horseback to establish a periphery the cattle were not to cross. The cattle looked fine, but an extra twelve hours on grass would get them into even better shape for market.

Ben directed Jed and the McLaughlin boys to stay with the cattle for a few hours while he, Roy, and Benjy rode into the village to make contact with the government agent.

The threesome rode to a small rise and looked down at the village of Rosebud. It was not an impressive sight. Below the low hills, several buildings were gathered together: the agent's office, his wood frame house, a church and workshop. Set off from the buildings was a large grouping of wood frame homes and teepees. Some were permanent; others provided temporary housing for the Indians who had journeyed in to get their supplies. Further off stood a large, well built corral with a small building alongside. This would serve as the agent's headquarters during the butchering of the cattle.

They rode past the corral and over to the agent's headquarters. Ben asked Roy to show Benjy around while he made the arrangements for the transfer of the cattle.

The agent's office was a dark, clean room, sparsely furnished with a desk and several chairs. Federal Indian Agent John Smith sat at a well-ordered desk. Smith was a thin man, dressed in black, who could have passed for a mortician or an austere preacher. He was a very disciplined and honest man, though honesty was not generally a trait of Indian agents. He was an autocrat, a man who would have his way, and his stoical Quaker background convinced him that he needed to change the lives of the Indian people who were his charges. He genuinely believed that if the Indians would dress and behave as white men, they too would share the bounties of this great country.

John Smith rose from behind the desk and held out a hand to Ben Talbert. "Mr. Talbert, we've been expecting you."

"Hello, Mr. Smith. We've just arrived and are camped above the village."

"Good," answered Smith in a businesslike manner. "We're in great need of beef and will take all you can supply."

"I believe you will be pleased with the stock," Ben returned. "They've spent a summer on grass and the journey didn't tax them."

"We're going to have a kill tomorrow at mid-morning. If you and your men could cut out fifty head and drive them to the pens, it would be most appreciated. I'll send up some of the Indian boys to drive the remainder to our grazing area."

"Fine. I'll see you in the morning then," Ben said as he rose to leave.

"Good day to you, Mr. Talbert," Mr. Smith said in a formal manner strange to these rough, untamed areas of the West.

Roy and Benjy wandered around the teepee encampment and talked to some of the Indians sitting outside the lodges. Roy spoke with Old Man Afraid of Horses, a Chief of the Sioux who invited Roy to sit and have a smoke with him. Benjy smiled and chatted with several Indian boys who patted him on the back in a friendly manner.

As he returned from his visit with the agent, Ben joined Roy and the Chief. The Chief said he had visited with old man DuMarce and that the Frenchman had given him a fine halter. Ben and Roy found that to be a strange gift.

Ben and Roy rose to leave and expressed their thanks for the visit. Old Man Afraid of Horses went into his lodge and brought out a fine, beaded tobacco pouch which he offered to Ben. Ben thanked him and told him that his gift to the Chief was back at his camp and that he would bring it to him tomorrow. Ben knew that in the Indian way, one should never accept a gift without giving one in return.

The old Chief smiled a toothless grin in anticipation of his gift from this great, white rancher.

Walking from the lodge, Roy asked Ben, "What gift?"

"I don't know," Ben answered. "I didn't expect him to give us anything. I'll think of something."

Ben yelled at Benjy who broke away from his new found friends with a promise to return.

The three mounted their horses and rode out to where the cattle were bedded down for the night.

***

The morning chill was felt by all. Ben sat up from his bedroll and pulled on his boots. He stood up and stretched before sauntering over to where Roy had the coffee already at a boil.

"Mighty cool this morning," Roy said to his old partner.

Ben could only shake his head in benumbed agreement.

The boys rolled out of their bedrolls and shook, trying to warm themselves, their teeth chattering in the chilly fall air.

"You boys come over and get yourselves something in those bellies that'll warm you over," Roy yelled over at the youngsters.

Jed, returning from the last watch, rode up to the stretching and yawning cowboys.

"You boys better get the cobwebs out, we've got a busy day afore us," Jed said in a teasing tone.

"How they lookin', Jed?" Ben asked.

"All's fine," Jed answered as he dismounted and took a plate of food from Roy.

The men and boys gathered around the fire and ate their breakfast, the men washing down the fare with piping hot cups of coffee. The group was so involved with their morning repast that they hardly noticed the two riders coming toward them until the pair were nearly upon them.

Severson, stopping with his drover before the group, said in a hardy tone, "Sorry to startle you boys. I know how I am until I've had my breakfast."

Ben and the group smiled sheepishly and Roy said, "I guess if'n you was snakes, you'd a bit us."

Severson laughed loudly and then said, "I stopped in the village and they said you was up on the ridge. I've got your horses picketed a mile or so from here."

"Get down and have a cup of coffee," Ben invited the men. "I'll saddle up and we'll ride out to take a look at them."

The two men dismounted and took cups of coffee from Roy.

"Mighty obliged," said the tall horseman.

Ben walked over to where the horses were grazing and caught and saddled Cyclone. He mounted his gelding and rode back to the fire.

The two horsemen remounted and stood ready to lead Ben to the remuda.

"Roy, Agent Smith will be sending up some boys to drive the rest of the cows in with the government herd. I should be back by that time and we'll drive the fifty head to the slaughter pens."

Roy acknowledged Ben's directive and started giving instructions to Jed and the boys, as Ben and the two horsemen rode off.

The three riders loped a mile or so before coming to a large group of horses guarded by three drovers. Around fifteen head were picketed, and the others were grazing contentedly on the tall grass.

Ben got off his horse and walked around the picketed horses. Ben saw that Severson had been true to his word: these horses were among the finest he had seen in a long time and would be good breeding stock. Among the picketed horses was a dapple grey gelding whose gentle nature caught Ben's attention.

Ben looked over the remaining herd. Even the slicks were of good quality and a few could be used in his breeding plans.

After reviewing the remuda for some time, Ben joined Severson by the camp fire.

"Well, Mr. Severson," Ben began, "I'll give you $50.00 a head for the picketed stock, $25.00 a head for the others and $15.00 per head for the slicks. By my calculations this comes to $660.00."

Severson sat in silence a moment before responding, "You're a might better at ciphering than I am but it sounds fair to me. You've got a deal."

The two men rose to their feet and shook hands.

"When do you plan to leave?" Ben asked.

"We thought we'd watch the festivities in the village and head out tomorrow morning."

"Good," Ben returned. "I'll have the money for you this afternoon and I'll send up someone to watch the horses."

"Fine," Severson said. "We'll keep an eye on them till then."

"One more thing," Ben asked. "I wonder if I can take that dapple grey with me now?"

"Sure thing," answered Severson.

***

The village was alive with people and the mood was festive. Small groups of women worked around fires, cooking sweet meats and fry bread. Boys played a game chasing a hoop with sticks. Men sat in circles, trading items and smoking long stemmed pipes.

Ben and Benjy rode up to Old Man Afraid of Horses' lodge and dismounted. A young man went into the lodge and in a moment the chief appeared, a large grin on his face. He greeted Ben in a friendly manner and Ben promptly presented him the young pony. Ben saw that the Chief was very pleased with the gift, and despite his name, did not seem to be afraid of it in the least. Ben did not know how the Chief had come by his name; perhaps he had acquired it as a child. The Chief accepted the gift graciously and then ducked into the lodge. He reappeared a moment later with a multi-colored horse blanket which he presented to Ben. Ben smiled his acceptance and the two men grasped each other's arms in friendship.

People now began to gather around the pens for the slaughter and butchering of the beef. The Chief invited Ben and his son to join him and together they walked to the count pen. Thirty head of cattle were milling around in the pen awaiting their fate. As Ben and the chief sat down with Mr. Smith, the agent gave a signal for the activities to begin.

Ten riflemen sitting on the fence began systematically shooting the cattle. They were obviously well-practiced in this task, as the majority of the cattle were dead before they hit the ground. After all the cattle were down, several of the riflemen finished off any cows still moving. Within seconds of the last shot, men and women scrambled into the pen, picking out their beef for butchering. The men, armed with long knives, began skillfully carving up the carcasses. The hide of the cows was cut away to be used for clothing and shoes. The beef were quartered and the large pieces were placed in baskets to be washed and salted later. Although clothing was supplied by the government, the Indians still prided themselves on making their own natural clothing. Many still could not get used to the hard shoes and boots of the white man.

The boys from the outfit showed just in time to see a special event. Three of the rangier, wilder cows had been kept in a small pen by themselves. Near the pen, six riders dressed in breech cloths and war paint, were seated on painted ponies. At a signal from the Chief, the cows were released and the riders began chasing them through the village. Armed only with bows and arrows, the warriors skillfully and quickly brought down the three cows. Dismounting their ponies, the warriors then slashed the throats of the wounded cattle. They smeared the gushing blood of the animals on their arms and torsos, and began dancing and chanting around about the fallen beasts.

Benjy was mesmerized by the sight. He made an effort to take in every sound, sight and smell so that he could give his mother and siblings a detailed report about the wonders he had witnessed.

The eventful afternoon continued with dances and games. Benjy and Billy went from group to group watching the festivities. The boys missed nothing, devouring sight and sound.

Ben settled with the Texas drovers and bid them on their way. He and Roy sat by the fire in the early evening and talked about the trip and their desire to get back to the ranch. A western man may travel and enjoy the sights he encounters, but there is something in his soul that makes him want to get back to the home place. That home place may involve hard work and struggle, but the place is his, and the pride he takes in it runs deep.

Ben rounded up the boys, their heads still whirling with excitement. He told them to saddle up and meet the men at the pens. Their faces fell. He told them not to fret; they both had done well and would be part of the drive next year. The promise revived their spirits.

Roy and Jed were mounted by the pens as Ben mounted Cyclone. The boys soon found them. Ben led the group of riders past Old Man Afraid of Horse's lodge and out of the village of Rosebud.

Chapter Nineteen

The trail between Deadwood and Ft. Pierre was a bumpy, axle-breaking track that swirled its way in a serpentine manner between the two western outposts. Kerlan had ridden this track for several days without incident. His only encounter had been with a wagon train of drovers carrying supplies and goods from Ft. Pierre to Deadwood. The midday sun now warmed Kerlan and his horse. The early morning frost had been chilling, and the warmth was a welcome change. Kerlan worried about the days ahead and wondered if he had truly made the right decision to go east.

His mind turned again to Kate. By now, she would be well on her way to New Mexico Territory. Kerlan's feelings were mixed. He had felt whole again in her presence, but the memory of how she had once left him, together with his current pressing work for Drummond, drove any tender thoughts from his mind.

Bursts of gunfire could be heard in the distance. Kerlan worked his gelding into a canter and moved toward the sound. As he came closer, he made out sporadic rifle fire. A shot. Another shot. A pause. Another shot.

He rode his horse up the crest of a hill just off the main trail and looked down into a small clearing. There he could see a single covered wagon. Under the wagon, two people were firing between the spokes of the wagon wheel at several mounted Indian braves who sat just outside of gunshot range. After every two shots, the braves would charge the wagon. As they were charging, the people at the wagon held their fire. Just before the braves reached the wagon, a shot again would ring out. The braves would swing out wide and return to their position just outside firing range. Kerlan realized that the people under the wagon were using breach loaded rifles capable of firing only once before reloading.

Kerlan moved across the crest of the hill to the opposite side of where the braves were stalking their kill. When he reached the other side, he spurred his horse into a full gallop down the hill. Before the Indians realized what was happening, he had moved quickly across the small clearing and to the other side of the wagon. Reaching the wagon, he dismounted as his horse came to a quick stop before the surprised onlookers.

Reaching across his saddle, he pulled his Henry from its scabbard. He faced a man, a woman and two small girls huddled below the wagon.

"Howdy, folks," Kerlan said, almost casually.

Relief at the arrival of this stranger quickly replaced the travelers' initial shock.

The Indians, upset that a new party had entered into the fight, charged angrily toward the wagon. Kerlan raised the back site on his Henry, aimed and fired. The lead brave fell hard from his painted horse. Smoothly, Kerlan ejected the spent shell and pulled another shell from the Henry's magazine into the chamber. A second shell was fired, and a second brave fell.

The third rider pulled around hard, looking at the ground where his two companions lay sprawled on the prairie. He galloped quickly back to the position where all three had sat moments before. The brave looked over the scene then suddenly began to scream in a yelping, birdlike manner. He worked himself into frenzy, tightening his legs around the horse's belly. He lowered his chest to the neck of the horse and drew his heels to the horse's loins, driving it forward.

The horse quickly moved through the gaits into a quick gallop toward the wagon. Kerlan pulled his rifle down for a moment. Both admiring and regretting the young brave's reckless charge. But finally he raised his rifle, aimed carefully, and squeezed off another round.

The young brave rolled off the back of the horse in a somersault and landed, hard, face and belly first, on the ground.

The family at the wagon watched the events in horrified amazement. The man had not even raised his rifle from the time Kerlan came upon the scene.

"I thank you, sir," he stammered. "I don't believe we would have come out of this alive."

Kerlan thought the same, but held his tongue. They looked young and inexperienced. Kerlan wondered if they would have the time to grow strong, and tough enough to endure what they would have to face out in the Far West.

"Where are you folks from?" Kerlan asked, breaking the awkward silence that had fallen upon them.

"Wisconsin," the young man said. "We are going to settle in Wyoming."

"Why aren't you with a wagon train?" Kerlan asked.

"We tried to get on but could not get our gear and wagon lined up to meet one in Minnesota. We had the choice of waiting till spring or going now and decided that our money wouldn't hold out. We decided to take our chances in the fall."

Kerlan decided that he wouldn't interfere or offer advice. People had to live their own lives and make their own mistakes. He wasn't one to tell people what they should or should not do. Regardless of chance or circumstance, a man had to do what he saw as fit and right for himself.

Kerlan nodded, "Well, I'm going out to bury those men. You go ahead and tend to your wagon and horses."

"We would be glad to have you stay with us tonight and have supper. I was able to shoot a couple of jacks this morning, and my wife makes a fine rabbit stew."

"Well, thank you," Kerlan replied somewhat taken aback. "I'd be honored to stay and eat with you tonight."

Kerlan took a shovel off the side of the wagon and walked out to where the three bodies were lying. The first two lay close together. They were boys in their late teens. The third, the youngster who had charged so gallantly, appeared to be about sixteen years old. They were lean, yet muscular, coppery, and handsome young men all, dressed in nothing but loin cloths, with war paint on their arms, legs and torsos. The bronze bodies of the young warriors stretched full out on the prairie. With certainty, they had been their parent's pride, and a young maiden's dream.

It was strange to see such a small, warlike group outside the reservation. But Kerlan knew that many of the young men, upset at their elders' acceptance of reservation life, yearned to lead the free life of their forefathers.

The braves' rider less horses stood, lonely sentinels, far out of the reach of the white man. Kerlan knew that it would be difficult to catch them, and that in any case they would find their way back to the reservation. The relatives of these young men would then at least know they would return no more.

After burying the three riders, Kerlan returned to the wagon. The woman was preparing the supper, and Kerlan sat down by the fire.

"Where are you going, sir, if I might ask?" the young man said.

"I'm heading toward Ft. Pierre."

"Ah, yes. We just went through there. We stopped for a day to gather supplies. Have you been there before?"

"No, I haven't," answered Kerlan, shortly, unwilling to reveal too much information.

After a hardy meal of rabbit stew Kerlan enjoyed a cup of coffee. While he prepared to leave, Kerlan found himself offering advice in spite of himself.

"It would be best if you traded those breach loads in and got yourself a repeater. I think if you would have thrown a little more lead at those braves they would have left you alone."

"Thank you, sir, for your advice. I admit I am new to this country and have a lot to learn."

Kerlan nodded. He hoped this country would give him enough time to learn it.

He mounted his horse and bid goodbye to the family. As he reached the top of the hill, he turned back to look and saw them huddled together, waving vigorously. He waved back and disappeared behind the rise.

Chapter Twenty

The lone rider sat upon his horse and looked down on the Bad River Ranch. To his eyes, the ranch looked like a prosperous place; a fine house, good out buildings and sturdy corrals. In the distance, a large herd of cattle grazed on the high prairie grass. The proprietor had done well.

Within that house, Irma pulled a tray of baked bread out of the coal black stove. As the aroma filled the kitchen, Irma wished Ben were around. He so loved the smell of fresh baked bread.

Suddenly, the door to the ranch house burst open and Sammy came rushing in.

"There's a rider coming, Ma," he exclaimed.

Irma wiped her fingers on her apron as she walked out onto the front porch. She squinted in the mid-day sun and tried to make out the identity of the person coming toward them. She had developed some skill in making out visitors at a distance. She knew it couldn't be their neighbor since he had dropped by to check on them just two days back.

When she still could not recognize the rider as he neared, Irma went into the house and returned to the porch with a Winchester rifle. She sent the children into the house and stood to meet the stranger.

The man seemed unthreatening enough, as he rode into the yard, but Irma took no chances. Operating the lever action, she placed a shell in the chamber.

The man rode up to the house and took off his hat.

"Good day, Ma'am," he said in a friendly, casual manner, ignoring the rifle.

"Hello," Irma returned guardedly.

"I was wondering, Ma'am, if this might be Ben Talbert's place. A man on the trail directed me this way."

"It is," Irma said nervously, the rifle quivering in her hands.

The stranger didn't speak for a moment, more hesitant.

The rider finally broke the uneasy silence.

"And would you be his wife?"

"Yes, I am," Irma answered, her voice unsteady. "Could I ask who you are and what business you might have with my husband?"

The man took a deep breath and answered, "I'm Ben's brother."

***

Kerlan sat at the kitchen table over the cup of coffee Irma had poured him. Irma cut up a large apple pie and set a piece in front of her newly discovered brother-in-law.

"Thank you," Kerlan said politely.

Irma sat silently in a chair at the other side of the table, watching as he ate. A thousand questions were running wildly through her mind, but she did not know where to begin.

"Ben's told me a lot about you. At least what he knew up until you left home. You were sixteen?"

"Fifteen," Kerlan corrected her.

"Fifteen," Irma repeated. "Ben said he admired your spunk – you being the younger brother. He never knew why you left though."

Kerlan didn't much care to rehash his past, but felt that Irma had the right to know.

"When Pa died, things changed. Ma decided to leave Red Wing and move to Springfield. She said us boys would work for Uncle Owen in the hardware store. I saw a future I didn't want being forced on me, so I decided to leave."

"Where did you go?" Irma asked, unable to restrain her curiosity.

"Down river to St. Louis. Worked on the barges for a time. Then signed up with a wagon train and came west."

"What did you do for a living?" Irma inquired further.

Kerlan felt ill at ease with the line of questioning and decided to try to put things on Irma's side of the wire.

"'Bout everything you could think of. The far West is a rough place and a man's got to move from job to job. Now what about you and Ben, how'd you end up out here?"

"It was Ben's dream," Irma answered. "We were living a happy enough life in Springfield when Ben came to me one evening with his plan to settle out West. We sold the store and Benjy and I went to live with the aunts in St. Paul while Ben and Roy came out to start the ranch. I'll admit I was hesitant at first, but I've come to love the life out here. It's hard, but there's a real feeling that everything is yours and that through your labors you can make life better."

"You've done well from what I can see," Kerlan answered with genuine admiration. "You've got a beautiful place here."

"What about you, Sam?" Irma used his name for the first time. "Are you married? Do you have any children?"

"Never was settled enough, I guess," Sam answered sheepishly.

As if to save him further embarrassment, Laura and Sammy rushed in the front door.

"Laura and Sammy, this is your Uncle Sam. Sam meet your niece and your namesake."

Sam said hello to the children and patted young Sammy on the head. He was uneasy with children, never having been around them much.

Irma broke up the awkward moment by asking in a cheerful tone, "Sammy, how would you like to show your uncle around the ranch yard?"

Sammy was delighted with his appointed task. He felt a natural affinity with the stranger, a kinship that sensed a shared history.

Sam followed the little fellow around the ranch yard and out buildings. He smiled and spoke encouragingly when young Sammy pointed something out to him.

His brother Ben had done well. The ranch was impressive. The large barn and corrals were well designed and built with close attention to detail.

The boy led Sam through the barn to a large corral of horses at its back. The youngster climbed on the fence and Sam leaned on the rail and admired the remuda.

"What's an uncle?" Sammy asked shyly.

The question startled Sam in its frankness. He gathered his thoughts and answered.

"Well, Son, an uncle would be a brother of your father. Your Pa and I are brothers."

The very thought put Sammy's mind in a whirl. "This man is to Pa what Benjy is to me," Sammy thought.

"Where you been?" Sammy persisted in questioning.

"That's a good question, Sammy," Kerlan answered philosophically.

The boy's gaze indicated that the answer was insufficient. Kerlan continued, "I've been out in the Far West making my living, but I'm here now, visiting my family."

The boy smiled and jumped down from the fence. He took his uncle by the hand and led him back toward the ranch house.

Chapter Twenty-One

The evening breeze was brisk as Sam sat on the ranch house porch smoking a cheroot. The autumn stillness and the lowing of the cattle in the distance lulled Kerlan into peaceful thoughts. He thought of Kate and of her journey down to Taos. She would be nearing the end of that journey and would soon be in the bosom of Alcalde Barela's hacienda.

Irma had been in the house settling down the children for the night. When she came out onto the porch, she startled Kerlan from his musings.

"Kids all bedded down?" he asked her.

"Yes. It's been a long and exciting day for them."

"You have some wonderful children there, Irma," Sam said. "You and Ben have a lot to be proud about."

Irma sat on a rocker next to Sam and took in the peaceful vista. They sat in silence for a time and let the evening's sounds and sights surround them.

As Sam crushed out his cigar on a handrail, Irma asked, "Did you ever settle anywhere for long, Sam?"

Sam was in a thoughtful mood and answered, "We had a place near Taos, New Mexico Territory for awhile. It was a little adobe and I guess it was the longest time I spent in any one place. I also had a cabin on the Pecos River."

"What's New Mexico like?"

"It's a different kind of place. Desert like, but there are running streams and mountains with snow on them. The plants are different. The animals are different. It's hard to describe. The sunsets are the most beautiful I've seen anywhere. The land is alive somehow, full of spirits."

Sam suddenly became embarrassed for going on so. Irma watched him and sensed how much her husband's brother was like him. His tender side was far beneath the surface and needed to be mined with care.

Sam felt the need to change the subject and searched his mind for a way out. Finally he said, "I appreciate the hospitality but would like to repay it somehow. What could I do around here to help you out until Ben returns?"

"You're family, Sam. You don't need to repay anything," Irma replied.

"I would like to do something. Ben won't be back for awhile, and I'd get bored just sitting around."

Irma could sense Sam's pride was involved in this and said, "Well, I do need to get into Ft. Pierre for some supplies. I would be grateful if you would take us in tomorrow with the buckboard."

"I'd be mighty pleased to," Sam answered with a satisfied voice.

"I'll go in now," Irma said quietly. "We'll head into town after breakfast."

"Fine," Sam answered. "Good night, Irma."

"Good night, Sam Kerlan," Irma returned with a smile.

***

Sam hitched up the buckboard and waited for Irma and the children to come out of the ranch house. The morning was cool, and Sam could see the breath in front of his face.

Irma and the youngsters came out of the house, Irma tightening a scarf about Laura's neck. Sam lifted the children into the back of the wagon and helped Irma into her seat. Climbing up next to her, Sam slapped the reins against the horse's flank and moved out of the ranch yard.

The path from the ranch down to the mouth of the Bad River was well worn. It was part of an ancient trail the Indians had taken west to the Black Hills. It was now worn by wagon wheels and horses hooves and was easily followed, a scorched path through the sea of prairie.

The children were talking quietly, pointing out the wonders of the day to one another. Irma sat quietly and smiled to herself. She enjoyed going into the small settlement of Ft. Pierre because it afforded her the female companionship that she sometimes missed since leaving Minnesota. While in Ft. Pierre, she and Mrs. Hagerty would often have tea together and talk about their children, the latest fashions, and who was doing what in and around Ft. Pierre. Mrs.

Hagerty received much of the information in the area and she took seriously her responsibility to pass this information along. The men folk would often joke that Mrs. Hagerty was a safe person to tell any dirt to, as it went in one ear and immediately out her mouth.

In what seemed like no time at all the buckboard reached Ft. Pierre. The little town was growing fast but was still being out paced by her sister city, Pierre, across the Missouri River. She remained the choice of the ranchers and freighters on the western side of the river and was a favorite of young cowboys, soldiers and travelers as Ft. Pierre seemed to turn a blind eye to many of the vices the good people of Pierre looked askance at.

Sam maneuvered the buckboard down the busy street. He could see several hotels and saloons, a couple of restaurants, a number of warehouses, a blacksmith shop, two dry goods stores and a dance hall. It seemed like a lively, active little town.

Irma directed Sam to Hagerty's Dry Goods. Sam helped her and the children down and told them he would be back in an hour. Sam moved up the street and dropped the buckboard off at the livery. He had been on the trail and away from civilization for some time, and didn't think Irma would deny him the pleasure of one glass of rye.

Kerlan walked up the dusty little main street and entered the first saloon he encountered. There were few occupants in the establishment at this time of day, and Kerlan had little trouble in getting a short glass of rye from the bartender.

He took his time with the drink for he knew it would be his only one. He seldom drank while charged with some responsibility, and he felt that the safety of his brother's family was the ultimate responsibility.

Finishing his drink he walked out of the bar and across the street to a dry goods store. He bought a bag of peppermint hard candy for the children, taking one himself to cover the scent of the whiskey.

He went back out onto the street and sat on a bench in front of the bank. Kerlan enjoyed coming into town now and then. He liked to watch the people: He was fascinated by their lives, what they did, and how they lived. But it was only a temporary pleasure. After a few hours, he would be ready to return to the high plains, with hulking mountains in the distance and a cool mountain stream running by.

Ft. Pierre was busy this fresh fall day. Ranchers and settlers were buying stores for the winter. Freighters on the Ft. Pierre-

Deadwood run were readying their teams for another journey across the wide expanse of prairie. A troop of soldiers was in town, moving up river toward Ft. Abraham Lincoln far to the north.

Kerlan watched this activity for a time. He checked his pocket watch and saw that he still had a good half hour to kill. He pulled his hat over his eyes and closed them, relaxed and let the warm autumn sun take away the chill of the day.

At times the shadows of passing people would cross over Kerlan. One of these hovered too long and Kerlan raised his hat and squinted at the figure standing over him. He automatically reached for his gun.

"No need to panic," Gil Stuart intoned in a steely voice. "We don't want to make a scene with all these blue bellies around."

Kerlan slowly let go of the grip of his pistol, and carefully sized up the situation. Gil Stuart was standing in a duster, cradling a Winchester in his arms. Sanchez was grinning toothlessly as he leaned against the horse rail.

"Didn't think I'd see you boys again," Kerlan said calmly, not allowing any fear to show through.

"If you would've given us a couple more days in the Hills you wouldn't have seen us at all, but you didn't so we were bound to meet again," Stuart came back in the same steady and deliberate way.

"Did you know I was heading this way or is this meeting by chance?" Kerlan asked.

"Nothing much comes from chance, Mr. Kerlan. If I'd have done what I had originally planned I would have been out of those Hills by the time you came looking for us. A mistake on my part, one that cost me dearly. As for our meeting again, the growth of a beard, a little visit to Deadwood, a few drinks with your simple minded companion and a man finds out things. It's not all that complicated."

Kerlan sensed that the conversation was coming to a close. He stood up directly in front of Stuart. The action took Stuart off guard, and although he didn't move his feet, he swayed back somewhat before standing perfectly still. The two men looked intently at one another for a short time before Stuart spoke.

"No need to leave. Why don't you come over to the saloon and join Sanchez and me for a drink?" Stuart asked in mock friendliness.

"Had one already," Kerlan responded coolly, "and in much better company."

Stuart smiled a hard smile as Sanchez chuckled foolishly.

"We'll let you go about your business, Mr. Kerlan. It is my hope that we will meet again soon."

"I'll go about my business when and if I choose. As for meeting again, I'd put money on it," Kerlan answered coldly, willing the meeting to its end.

Stuart gazed at Kerlan for a time before signaling Sanchez and moving cautiously up the street.

Chapter Twenty-Two

Sam Kerlan made straight for the livery and readied the team for travel. Irma and the children were outside the dry goods store and he hurriedly loaded them and their goods into the wagon.

"What's wrong, Sam?" Irma said, noticing her brother-in-law's preoccupied demeanor.

"Oh, nothing, Irma," Sam lied. "I was just watching the sky in the west. Looks like we could get a little rain or snow tonight, and I thought we'd better head back toward the ranch."

"There is a dampish feeling in the air," Irma agreed. "I worry about Ben and the boys in such weather. They should be home soon by Ben's original calculations."

Sam heard her, but his mind was on getting out of town unobserved by Stuart and Sanchez. He would have to be careful on the trail, double back once in a while and make sure they were not followed. He didn't want Irma to notice anything unusual so he tried to keep up a light mood.

"You said that this is Benjy's first trip with his Pa?"

"Yes," Irma answered, happy to be asked about her family. "He was really hoping to go this time and Ben surprised us all by allowing it. Benjy really loves the ranch, horses, everything about our life out here. He's so much like his father, but you know something, he looks like you. Has your coloring."

Sam was taken back by this comment. As a man without children, it was a pleasant thought that someone should look like him. He'd always felt that he would like to have children of his own, especially a son. His life, however, had not permitted such a luxury.

Little Sammy, complaining of the cold, climbed up into the bench of the buckboard. His mother engulfed him in her huge cloak to warm him. After Sammy was comfortable, Irma continued the conversation.

"It's none of my business, Sam, but why did you change your name?"

"Well, you know that Kerlan is my Mother's maiden name and was given to me as a middle name. When I signed up to work a river boat I signed Samuel Kerlan Talbert. Well, when I was hired the Captain called out "Sam Kerlan" and I was known by that for the several months I worked the river. When I left the river, I just continued to use it, I guess. I don't know why."

The explanation seemed to satisfy Irma, but it was not the truth. The river was a rough place, the Far West even rougher, and he had had to do things that the conservative people of Minnesota would not have approved of, and he was making his way in a harsh land and building a reputation for himself. He just felt it was better if his family didn't know that he was becoming one of the West's most noted gunmen.

Sam moved the buckboard into some trees by the river and stopped the team of horses.

"Irma, I want to climb that knob of a hill and get a gander out west to see if those storm clouds are building. You and the children wait here and I'll be right back."

In truth Sam wanted to gaze back on the trail out of Ft. Pierre to see if they were being followed. The fear rising up in his heart was unusual, since so much more was at stake this time. He had his brother's family with him and was charged with their safety. Lord help Stuart and Sanchez if they endangered Ben's family. The wrath of hell would befall them; Kerlan would fight like a beast from the underworld to protect them.

From the hill's crest, he looked back along the Bad River into Ft. Pierre. He could see no sign of horse or rider. He could look out on the naked prairie, so he knew Stuart was not attempting to follow them. But he stayed on the hill for some time, just to make sure.

As Sam walked down the hill he heard a sweet voice fill the air. Irma was singing, and the children were sitting on the front bench listening contentedly to her. "Irma, I swear you're gonna put these horses asleep with your lullaby," Sam said in a kidding manner.

Irma and the children laughed heartily at the thought. Sam climbed up in the wagon, put Laura on his knee, and moved the wagon out from the trees and back on the river road to the ranch.

***

After a full breakfast and several cups of coffee, Sam went out to the barn to saddle up his roan. Irma had mentioned she was worried about the cows foraging too far from the ranch. Sam said he would be glad to ride out and check on them.

It was a chilly morning, though the sun was shining brightly. The previous night's storm had left a light coating of snow on the ground and the sun's reflection made the day all the more bright.

Sam mounted his horse and rode out of the ranch yard. This early morning ride involved more than checking on a few cows. Sam wanted to scout out the area and to be sure that Stuart and Sanchez had not discovered his whereabouts. He did not care for his own safety as he did for the security of his brother's family. He didn't want to bring his violent life to their doorstep.

Sam put the roan in an easy canter and watched the horizon. In a short time he started to encounter Ben's cattle. They were spread out in a valley between two bends of the river and seemed content and secure.

Sam rode his horse up a large hill and dismounted. From this height he could follow the river toward Ft. Pierre and see west for miles over the unending plain.

He crouched down, holding the reins of his horse in his hands. A multitude of thoughts were running through his brain. Meeting his brother's family had moved him, though he would show his emotions to no one. Now he wondered about Ben and his reaction to his visit. Would he accept his prodigal brother as easily as Irma and the children had accepted him?

He thought again of Kate. Could they regain the life they had together in New Mexico? Could he leave his past behind him and start anew? Would his past let him? The horse nuzzled Sam's back and brought him back to the world around him. He stood up and looked out onto the mesmerizing prairie, an expanse so large and wide it seemed to engulf him. Land and sky, open and unending. It made his worries seem small, and that comforted Kerlan.

Sam got up on his roan, breathing the fresh, cool air. The coolness cleared his head and heart and he nudged his horse back down the hill.

Chapter Twenty-Three

Benjy Talbert cantered alongside the remuda to where his father was riding at its head. He pulled up reins and came to a walk beside his father's horse.

"How you doing, Son?" Ben asked.

"Good, Pa. Lookin' forward to some of Ma's cooking."

"Me too. It's good to get out on the trail now and then, but you know what the best part of it is? Coming home! Makes you realize what you got."

"Pa?" Benjy began, struggling to find the right words. "I was wondering, when we get home, I mean. Well, Billy sure likes working the cows and all. Bobby is heading straight for Ft. Pierre, he told me that, but, well, Billy doesn't know where he'll go."

"I know, Son, I've been thinking along the same lines. Jed too, finds it hard to keep busy in the winter when trapping plays out. I've decided to offer both Jed and Billy full time work. I haven't told you, but I'm buying the Dempsey place and I'll put Jed and Billy over there. They can take care of the herd over the winter. You, me and Roy will keep the horses on our place and work them through the winter."

Benjy knew his Pa would come through. He was so filled with happiness that he could barely contain himself.

"Can I tell Billy?" he exclaimed.

"Sure, Son, you go ahead."

Benjy dug his heels in his pony's flank and made off to the back of the remuda to pass on the good news. Roy, noticing the boy's excitement, rode his horse around the remuda to Ben's side.

"What's got the youngin' stirred up?" he asked.

"I told him about our idea of keeping Jed and Billy on full time. He and Billy have become pretty close and he was excited to tell the boy."

"Both Jed and the McLaughlin boy are good hands," Roy commented. "I gave Jed the news yesterday and he was real pleased.

They can do some fixin' on the Dempsey place and keep track of the herd. We'll have our hands full with all these horses."

Suddenly, movement off in the distance caught Ben's attention. Three riderless Indian ponies were making their way south. The ponies wore bridles and two had blankets on them.

"What do you make of that?" Ben asked.

"Don't rightly know. My guess would be that the owners of those ponies no longer walk the good earth."

"Yea," Ben returned. "There's no horse as loyal as an Indian's pony. They somehow lost their riders and are making their way back to the reservation."

They watched for a time until the Indian ponies sensed them, and the fear of the unknown sent them to a gallop, still southerly but away from the men and remuda.

***

When the drovers caught sight of the Bad River Ranch their hearts lifted. The boys gave out several yelps of glee. Ben felt like joining them but held it in.

Benjy cantered around the remuda and pulled up to where his father and Roy were leading the horses.

"Can I gallop in, Pa?" he asked.

"Yea, Son, go ahead," Ben answered. "The sooner your Ma knows you're ok, the better I'll feel."

With this permission Benjy put his pony into a freewheeling gallop toward the ranch house. Ben and Roy watched in amusement.

"That boy sure can ride," Roy said.

"He had a couple good teachers," Ben said and smiled at Roy.

The remaining men herded the horses steadily toward the ranch. They were all looking forward to warm baths and home cooked meals.

The horses began to get nervous as they neared the ranch buildings. Having been free on the plains for months they would fight against being brought into corrals, and so Ben told the boys to be extra watchful.

The men skillfully worked the horses, moving them through the ranch yard to where Benjy was standing by the open gate of the large corral. As Ben waved to Irma and the children on the porch he noticed a stranger standing next to them. He was too busy, however, getting the horses into the corral to ponder his identity.

Benjy closed the gate behind the last riders. The drovers dismounted inside the enclosure and Benjy let them out one by one. Ben came through the gate and tied Cyclone to the corral fence. He shook off some dust and then looked toward the ranch house. Irma and the youngsters were coming toward him, the children running until their father scooped them up in his arms. He kissed both of them and then set them down on the ground.

Irma walked up to Ben and the two embraced.

"Howdy, Sweetheart. Glad to have us back?"

Irma was clearly choked up. She smiled and wiped tears from her eyes. Benjy came over to them and she put her arm through his and walked her two men toward the ranch house.

"I have someone I want both of you to meet," she informed them.

As they neared the house, the stranger Ben had noticed when they came into the yard stepped off the porch and stood before them. He took off his hat and waited until the three reached him.

"Ben," Irma said calmly and deliberately, "this is your brother."

Ben was speechless. He had not seen his brother in years. The two men shook hands, staring at one another. The awkwardness was broken suddenly by Roy yelling, "The horses are scared, and I think they're going to rush the fence!"

Sam followed Ben over the fence and into the corral. Both men knew what they were about. They talked in an easy manner to the running horses and got them moving in a circular fashion inside the corral. They continued this for some time, talking in assured tones to the horses as the animals ran off their nervous energy. In a short time, the horses were trotting around the corral, and then quickly settled down to a walk. Sam expertly roped a buckskin mare that seemed to be stirring up the other horses, taking her to the corral gate and giving her to Roy. With the mare removed, the other horses seemed to settle down and become acclimated to their new surroundings.

Sam and Ben stood together at the corral gate, recovering from the excitement.

"Thanks for the help." Ben spoke the first words in twenty years to his brother.

"Glad to," Sam answered, not knowing what to say next.

They were saved by Irma calling everyone in to supper. She had set up the long table in the kitchen for the adults and a smaller one in the larder for the young ones. Everyone on the cattle drive sat down to the meal, with the exception of Bobby McLaughlin. He collected his pay and made straightaway for Ft. Pierre and civilization as he knew it.

The adults conversed about the ride down to Rosebud, but both Sam and Ben remained silent. Both men cast furtive glances at one another as they ate. They were eyeing each other's mannerisms, searching the past to remember a brother who had seemed lost forever.

After the meal Ben told Roy to take Jed and Billy up to the Dempsey place and get them set up. Benjy was sent out to the barn to care for the saddle horses, exhausted after the long ride. Sam offered to help and followed his nephew out the door.

Irma was cleaning up after the meal, and Ben watched out the window at his son and brother heading toward the barn.

"I can't believe it, Irma. I can't believe he's here. It's Sam alright. A man knows his own brother, but I don't know what to say to him. It's been so long."

"You'll know what to say when the time comes. You both have a lot to talk about."

"What has he told you so far?" Ben asked.

"Not all that much. He's not married and has no children. He's been out in the Far West."

"How'd he find us after all this time?"

"I don't rightly know. But Ben, you can ask him all these things. He's come a long way to see you."

"Twenty years," Ben said almost to himself, continuing to stare out the window. "Twenty years."

Chapter Twenty-Four

Twilight settled itself in among the small valleys, touched the low hills and colored the meandering Bad River in hues of gray. The Bad River had gotten its name from Indians who had camped along its bank for millennia. Legend has it that after days of rain a flash flood had carried away an Indian encampment, and from that day forward the Indians in and around the area called the river bad.

Ben sat on the front porch, drawing heavily on his pipe. He could hear voices in the barn; the voice of his son and the voice of his brother speaking in low, friendly tones. The conversation seemed animated, and Ben wondered how his normally taciturn son had come to feel so at ease with this stranger.

The two came out of the barn and were walking toward the house. Ben caught a fragment of the conversation; the man telling the boy about a big hole in the ground in Arizona Territory folks said was hit years ago by something from the sky.

When they saw Ben on the porch, the man grew quiet. They walked up to the steps to join him.

"Pa, Uncle Sam here says that there's a place in Arizona Territory that was hit by a falling star, a hole so big you could put a mountain in it. Said he walked to the floor of the hole himself."

"I heard tell of such a place," Ben answered, working to keep up a normal conversation and put his son and brother at ease.

"He's also been to the large canyon on the Colorado. Said that when you look down at the river it looks like a mark you would make on the ground with a stick."

"Son, you go in the house now," Ben instructed. "Been a long day and you need your rest."

"Yes, sir. Goodnight, Uncle Sam. See you in the morning."

"Goodnight, Benjy."

The boy went into the house. Ben sat uneasily, puffing on his pipe. He was still amazed at how fast this man had won over his son

Sam stood just as uneasily. The two were silent for a time before Ben spoke.

"Sit down if you want."

Sam climbed the stairs and took a rocker across from Ben. He reached in his waistcoat for a cheroot. He offered one to Ben who declined.

Sam lit his cigar and the two men sat, neither knowing where to begin. Ben, again, broke the stalemate.

"Irma says you been out West."

"Yup," Sam replied.

Another long silence engulfed them. They were men who had been raised together, had played as pirates along the mighty Mississippi, had teased each other and comforted each other. At that time, they had been able to speak to one another with ease.

"Gilly," Ben said. "One night on the trail as I watched the herd, I thought of little Gilly."

The name stirred something deep in Sam Kerlan. The name of the little black boy from his past brought back a flood of memories that seemed to overwhelm him. He felt himself begin to sweat, his body started to shake and, to his own astonishment, he began to cry.

The sight of this man leaning over his chair, his back shaking, and his face buried in his hands, startled Ben at first. This was not some stranger off the prairie, this man was his brother, his flesh and his blood. Their bond was the love of their parents and of their childhood together.

Ben stood up from his chair and went over to Sam and placed a hand on his shoulder. Sam sat up and looked into the face of his brother.

"I'm sorry, Ben, I don't know what caused that."

"It's me that's sorry. When Irma introduced us I was so shocked I didn't know what to do."

Sam stood up and he and Ben embraced.

"Welcome home, little brother," Ben said through his own tears.

***

Morning came early, particularly for the two brothers who had spent half the night visiting, making up for lost time.

After an early breakfast they decided to take a ride out on the range and check the cattle. Benjy asked to go with them, and Ben gave his permission.

Benjy saddled up the three horses and waited for his father and uncle at the barn. Ben and Sam came out of the ranch house and took in the new morning air. They walked over to where Benjy and the horses were waiting.

"That's a fine horse you got there, Uncle Sam," Benjy said as he handed the reins of the roan to his uncle.

"Thanks, Benjy," Sam said as he took the reins. "Yea, we been through a lot together. Don't think I've ever had a better horse. You got some pretty good stock around here yourselves."

"We've been doing some selective breeding," Ben returned. "Trying to keep up the speed while toning down the disposition. We need good cutting horses with the tight spaces around here. Sometimes you have to turn a cow on a knob of earth so small you could spit off the edge of it."

The three mounted up and rode out of the ranch yard. They trailed their horses for a time but Benjy's pony was feeling jumpy in the frosty morning air and was anxious to run.

"Pa, is it ok if'n I run him a bit. He needs to settle down."

"Go ahead, Son, but watch your footing," Ben said.

Benjy gave his horse some rein and the little cow pony sprung into a canter. Ben and Sam watched the youngster and horse move away.

"You've got quite a boy there, Ben. Something to be real proud of."

"Yea. I guess I couldn't ask for more in a son. He likes ranch life. I see him taking over for me one day. What about you, Sam, why no family?"

"I don't know. Moved around too much, I guess. I thought once I would settle down, but that changed."

"It's not too late, you're young yet," Ben encouraged.

"Yea, you never know. I guess I'd give my right arm for what you got."

In the distance, a lone rider made his way at a run over the white prairie. Ben and Sam squinted into the brightness of the day to make out who was riding toward them.

"It's Benjy," Sam said. "He's coming in a terrible hurry."

The two dug heels into their horses' flanks and galloped toward the boy. As they neared they could see he was in a panic. In a short time, they met the boy, whose horse stopped just short of charging into them.

"What's the trouble, Son," Ben asked anxiously.

Benjy sat on his horse trying to catch his breath. "Riders," Benjy said, breathing hard and barely able to speak. "They were shooting at me."

Sam pulled his Henry rifle from its saddle scabbard and injected a shell into its chamber all in the same smooth motion.

"Ben, take the boy and head back toward the ranch. I'll slow these fellas down a bit."

"But you'll be outnumbered, Sam," Ben exclaimed.

"Do it, Ben. Take the boy to safety." This order was given with such authority that Ben could do nothing but obey it. He watched as his brother spurred his horse into a gallop toward the unknown riders.

Ben and his son rode away toward the ranch at a fast pace. All the while Ben was listening for gunshots. Yet as time passed, he heard nothing. He and Benjy rode up a small rise and came to a stop, looking back at where they had been. A group of riders were making for them. Benjy started to kick his horse and run away, but his father continued to watch the riders.

"Hold it, Son. I know those men. That's Joe Copper and his outfit, and your uncle is with them."

Ben was baffled, and could only wait until the riders joined them.

"These men say they know you, Ben," Sam began when they rode up. "They're out looking for some cattle rustlers and they mistook Benjy for one of them."

"Real sorry about that, Ben," Joe Cooper said apologetically. "Tom here is a little trigger happy."

"He's damned lucky he isn't a good shot," Ben said coldly.

"I am a good shot," spoke up a spindly little cowboy with few front teeth and a vacant, leering grin, "and I'd got the little shit if Joe here wouldn't have pulled me up."

"Why you little bastard," Ben said and moved his horse at the man. Sam and Joe Cooper put their horses between them.

"Take it easy now, Ben," Joe Cooper said, "and you, Tom, you ignorant son-of-a-bitch, you keep your mouth shut."

Ben was still fuming but the two horsemen kept him from doing anything. Sam put his hand on his brother's shoulder.

"Easy now, Ben, this gentleman was just doing his duty as part of this posse, now weren't you," Sam said turning his horse to the toothless, unshaven cowboy.

"Yes, I was," Tom said arrogantly. "How was I to know that this little runt wasn't one of them rustlers?"

"I agree with you, Tom, we all must do our duty."

With these words Sam flipped his .44 Henry over, grabbing it with both hands by the barrel and swinging it with force, hitting the cowboy full in the face with the gun's stock. The force of the blow knocked the rider off the back of the horse and onto the ground. He lay in an unconscious, crumpled mass, blood pouring off his face onto the ground.

"Now there was no need for that," Joe Cooper said, stunned at the sudden action.

"Yes, there was," Sam returned.

Sam's words were so decisive that they put an end to any further discussion.

"He is a dumb bastard. I should have done that to him long ago," Cooper agreed.

Ben looked at his brother, half in appreciation and half in shock at the quick, sure, and cruel way he handled the situation. Perhaps the cowboy was lucky. In his own anger over the safety of his son, he might just have killed the man.

Sam looked at Ben and his gaze seemed to say, "I might just have saved you from a murder charge, big brother."

"I'll have to send a man back with cow-dip here," Joe Cooper continued. "I wonder if you would like to join us. We're after some rustlers and had their trail until late yesterday."

Ben knew his duty as a fellow range man. He knew he would have to go with the men.

"I'll join you, Joe. Sam, maybe you and Benjy should ride back to the ranch. I'll join you later after we catch these men."

"I'm coming along," Sam said. "It's the least I can do after what I did to his man."

"OK," Ben said, agreeing quickly. "Benjy, you ride straight for the ranch and let Ma and Roy know what we're doing. We should be back in a few days."

"Yes, Sir," the boy answered and turned his pony toward home.

"OK, let's go," Ben said and the group of horsemen rode off toward the western sky.

Chapter Twenty-Five

The riders moved in a northwesterly direction for most of the day. Ben watched as Sam slowly but assuredly took command of the group. His skills at tracking became obvious to the other men and by mid-afternoon they had picked up the trail of the cattle thieves.

Sam led the men to a stand of cottonwoods near a small pond, a well known watering hole in the area. He dismounted and walked around the area. It was apparent to all that the site had been a campground in the last couple of days. A small enclosure of stones where a fire had been lit still remained.

Sam walked back to the waiting riders.

"They left here yesterday morning. Two or three of them as near as I can make out. They have a small herd of cows and a few loose horses. If they're our men, they don't seem to be in any hurry."

"Why do you say that?" Joe Cooper asked.

"From all indications they came here the previous day and lingered until late morning before leaving. If they're thieves, they are lazy and slow ones."

"How far out ahead of us are they?" Ben questioned.

By now he fully trusted his brother's tracking skills.

"The cows will slow them down unless they get rid of them. I'd say we could catch up with them late tomorrow or the next day."

"You say they have some horses?" Joe Cooper interrupted. "That's a hanging offense in my book."

"It's a hanging offense in everybody's book, Joe," Ben answered him, "but you don't know, they might be slicks. Besides, we'll let the authorities do the hanging."

Joe Cooper did not argue the point, but Ben and Sam could tell he was not in agreement. Sam mounted his horse.

"Let's go, boys," he said, and the group followed him out of the small oasis on the prairie.

The riders moved steadily across the prairie toward the setting sun. Sam dismounted from time to time to cut for sign, and ensure that they were staying on the right trail.

As the day's shadows drew longer, Sam searched for a site to make camp. He pulled up and surveyed the terrain.

"We'll make for that little arroyo and set up camp," he informed the men in a matter of fact manner.

"That little what?" Joe Cooper asked, puzzled.

Kerlan had used the southwestern lingo, forgetting where he was for the time being.

"Sorry, we'll camp in that deep cut, out of the wind," he said to his fellow travelers.

Joe Cooper continued to look puzzled, but directed his men to follow this stranger's instructions.

Ben started a fire and Joe Cooper took some provisions out of his saddle bags and began fixing the evening meal. The other men settled down by the fire with the exception of Kerlan. He stood above the camp and watched the western sky.

Ben called to him to join them for the meal, and Sam came down from the rise. Joe Cooper handed him a plate of grub.

"Ben here tells me that you two are brothers," Cooper said in a friendly tone. "Where'd you learn to scout like that, in the Army?"

"No," Sam answered politely, but clearly not wishing to reveal much about his past. "Done a little out west. Pretty sparse out there, and I guess you realize when someone's crossed your path."

The answer seemed to mollify him so Cooper returned to the previous topic.

"Ben, what if these fellas have horses? Don't you think we should hang'em and be done with it? That's what they do up Cheyenne River way."

"Joe, I've known you for some time. I agree that horse thieves must be dealt with harshly, but I don't want to be judge and jury to any man, regardless of the offense. I say we have to take them back to Ft. Pierre and let the authorities handle it."

"I know, Ben," Joe Cooper came back, "but out here we have to handle it ourselves. There's no law out here. The government says its reservation, but people ignore it. We're the law here and we have to do something."

"There's no law now, Joe, but there will be. Maybe not next year, or in five or ten years, but there will be law, and until that time we must use what little law we have."

"Well, I guess you're right," Joe Cooper said grudgingly. "But I'd sure hate to see some horse thief go free."

Sam placed a few sticks on the fire and the rising flames seemed to put the argument to rest. The men watched the crescendo of flames and let the silence of the night overcome them.

***

Ben stirred from a restless sleep. The night had been a cold one, and he was chilled to his very marrow. He sat up and could see the other men bundled against the frigid air. Inside the stone enclosure he could see the remnants of the fire which were as cold as he was.

He got up stiffly and stretched, trying to get some circulation to his near frost-bitten appendages. He gathered up some sticks and began to build a fire. He looked over to where Sam had set out his horse blanket the night before and to his surprise did not see him. He gazed toward the horses and could see that Sam's roan was gone.

Joe Cooper also shook himself from a fitful sleep. He sat on his bedroll for a moment, stunned by the coldness of the morning.

"Damned cold," was all he could utter as he steeled himself for the chillness of the day.

Ben greeted Joe with a question. "You didn't see Sam head out this morning?"

"Hell no, Ben, where did he go?"

"I don't rightly know unless he set out to find the trail. I'm sure he'll be back soon," Ben said, though within himself he was not at all so sure.

The other riders stretched and grumbled about the cold night and the crispness of the new day. Ben got a pot of coffee brewing and reheated the previous night's fare. The group stood around and stared at the fire, as if pleading with it to end the misery of the morning.

After the men got a couple cups of coffee and some feed into themselves, their attitudes seemed to improve. Joe Cooper sat down beside Ben who was tending the fire.

"Where's that brother of yours?" A slightly worried tone in his voice, not sure what was happening.

"I don't know, Joe, but he must have lit out early. He should be showing up soon."

"If he doesn't, we'll have to head out without him," Joe said flatly.

Ben knew this to be true and acknowledged it by his silence.

After the meal the men readied their gear for the day's ride. Both Ben and Joe Cooper tried to prolong this activity as long as they could, but the other men were growing impatient and eventually they knew they could wait no longer for Sam.

"Well," Ben said, "we'd better move out. I'm sure Sam will join up with us later."

Joe Cooper nodded in agreement, and he and the rest of the men mounted their horses. Ben searched the western horizon one more time as the group of riders left the campsite.

Both Ben and Joe Cooper would readily admit that they were not the finest trackers in the West. After a few hours in the saddle the group seemed to lose their focus. Ben was worrying about Sam, while Joe Cooper and his men were growing restless with their seemingly directionless movement.

About the time Ben began to think he would have a mutiny on his hands, they spotted a movement on the far hills. They rode closer to investigate, but the brightness of the sun against the snow-covered ground made the movement hard to decipher.

At last, Ben could make out that the sight before them was a group of animals of some kind. As they moved closer, he could pick out riders.

"Looks like cattle and drovers," Joe Cooper said, stating the obvious.

The group of riders sat on their horses as the men and animals moved toward them. As they drew closer, Ben strained his eyes on one particular figure suspended between the blue sky and white earth.

"By God, it's my brother," he exclaimed.

The riders dug heels into their mounts and rode out to intercept. They rode around the small herd of cows that were being trailed by Sam and two cowboys. One of the cowboys was wearing a sling on one arm.

"What the unholy hell is going on here?" Joe Cooper said as the group rode up to Sam.

"I thought I'd let you boys sleep in this morning," Sam said cheerfully.

"Who are these two?" Cooper asked, gesturing toward the two forlorn looking cowboys on either side of the herd.

"Well, they're the sorriest couple of cattle rustlers I ever came upon. If they had a brain between them they would have passed up this rangy little bunch of cows."

Joe Cooper directed two of his men to watch over the herd. He and the third man brought the two hapless rustlers together and guarded them jealously.

Sam and Ben trailed behind this activity, chuckling at the spectacle.

"I'm sure Cooper and his boys will make this whole affair sound more exciting than it was," Ben said to his brother. "You know, though, that you shouldn't have gone out alone, you never know what you might have run into."

"Well," Sam returned, "I could tell by the tracks that we were trailing a couple of boys that didn't know hens from roosters. I thought that if I led this bunch in to them, someone was going to get hurt. Besides, I was freezing last night, I couldn't sleep."

Ben could see his brother's reasoning. They followed Cooper's bunch from a distance, slightly embarrassed to be thought a part of it.

Chapter Twenty-Six

The snow encased prairie made the west river country seem bigger, nearly endless. The harsh weather also made an already dangerous land all the more treacherous.

As they rode, Ben related to Sam the story of a ranch hand up on the Moreau who went out one morning into deep snow in search of stray cows. The snow had completely covered two hills. As he rode out between the knobs of these hills, the snow pack gave way and just swallowed him up. As the snows slowly melted away in the spring they found the man still in his saddle, a look of terror frozen on his face.

Sam shuddered at the story, which he found amusing in a horrible sort of way. They were still trailing the riders and cattle and were coming to the point where the group had originally met.

Joe Cooper rode back to them and pulled his horse alongside Ben's.

"Well, I guess this is where we part company. We'll take the cattle back to their owners' if'n you boys would like to take these two into Ft. Pierre?"

Cooper had apparently abandoned his notion of a hanging; both Ben and Sam sensed that he too found some humor in the situation.

"Thanks for your help fellas," he said after the two agreed. "Maybe some day we can go out after some real desperados."

Ben and Sam waved and watched as the horsemen rode off with the cattle. They joined the two rustlers who sat forlornly on their horses watching their departure.

"Boys, you have a rendezvous with the law in Ft. Pierre," Ben said to them, shaking them from their listlessness.

"What do you think they'll do to us? We didn't steal those cows, we found them."

"Well," Ben interrupted, "I don't think that the authorities will believe you're career bandits. We'll put a good word in for you, and I think they'll go easy. You're just lucky you didn't find horses."

***

Sam put in a good word for the cattle rustlers in Ft. Pierre. He did not have to argue his case too aggressively, though. Anyone could see that the two combined had no more sense than a buffalo calf.

Having done their duty, Sam and Ben decided to stop and have a hot meal, something they had missed the last two days out on the range. They entered a hotel that offered dining room services and sat at a table near the window. The waitress brought them coffee and informed them of the daily special.

Sitting back in his chair, Ben looked knowingly at his younger brother.

"I believe I have an inkling what you've been doing out West," he said in a controlled, poker table voice.

"Oh, yea," Sam came back slowly. "You finally figured out that I wasn't a sheep herder."

Ben laughed out loud. He then shook his head as if trying to deflect the humorous comment.

"Your ability as a tracker, the way you took charge of me and those men; it would be my guess that you're pretty handy with a pistol. Would I be right?"

"I guess you would, Ben," Sam admitted. "I never tried to cover up what I've done for a living. I've made my living with the skills I acquired honestly. I can't say I've not always done the right thing, but I've tried to be on the side that had the law behind it, although out west that sometimes wasn't the good side."

Ben sipped at his coffee and listened. His long silence began to disturb Sam. Though he wasn't always proud of his past, he refused to apologize for it, not even to his only brother.

"Sam," Ben began, finally breaking the silence. "I'm not going to cast any judgments on you or your life. I'm no one to do that. Out West we're all interlopers in a way. I started a ranch on what is still legally Indian land. I didn't know it at the time I bought it, but ignored it when I did. I made it my own. I know that life is hard and that compromises have to be made."

Sam nodded, accepting his brother's comments. The waitress brought over two large platters of food, and the brothers' dug in.

"What about this Indian land, what's going to happen?" Sam asked.

"Well," Ben began after swallowing a mouthful of food, "when we first came out here most of the white ranchers had some connection with the Indians, either married to them or partners with them. A lot of them were French. I bought my place from a Frenchman who was married to a Sioux woman. At first, they raided me a couple of times, not doing much harm, just taking a few head of cows now and then. The army came through the second year and told me to get out but never came back to enforce it. At the time, the Indians were being moved to permanent villages except for a few hold outs. After I started to supply beef to them, they kind of left me alone."

"What about your deed, is it any good?" Sam asked.

"Not worth the paper it's written on," Ben said, laughing. "That's why I've hedged and bought some land on the other side of the Missouri. There's talk of a bill in Congress to open up the reservation. If that happens, I'll be able to get sure title."

"Seems like a risky venture," Sam responded.

"No, it's just a matter of time. With the road through to Deadwood and other ranchers moving in, there's no way they can turn back the clock."

After they finished their meals, Sam offered and Ben accepted a cigar and the two sat back for a smoke. After a few moments Ben began again.

"There's a future out here. Statehood is only a few years away. There's plenty of grass to raise cattle and horses. There are good markets with the Indians and the army. There's talk of a rail line all the way to the Chicago stockyards. Think of it, beef for Chicago, Minneapolis and points east. A man can make a future for himself out here."

Sam had a suspicion that the man his brother was thinking of was none other than himself. The idea made him nervous, and he shifted in his chair. It made him especially uneasy because he had already been considering it himself.

Ben could sense his brother's edginess. He decided to push ahead.

"What I've been thinking, Sam, well, why don't you join us? You could settle down and build something for yourself. How about it?"

The straightforwardness of the proposal took Sam off guard. He didn't know what to say and took another long draught on his cigar to buy some time.

Ben waited anxiously for a response while Sam cleared his throat. "Can I think about it?" he finally managed.

"Sure," Ben said, respecting Sam's uncertainty. "We'll discuss it later."

They paid for their meal and strolled out of the restaurant and down the street toward the livery.

"I wanted to ask you something," Ben said. "Those rustlers, they had horses with them, didn't they?"

"Yep, they sure did," Sam came back, "and they were the mangiest swaybacks you ever come across. They were slicks, anyway, belonged to anybody. Nobody would want them."

"Or want to be hanged for them," Ben said looking at his brother in admiration.

Chapter Twenty-Seven

As a cinder shot out of the dying fire, Sanchez stirred in his sleep. Gil Stuart, staring hard at the glowing embers, blinked his eyes and shook his head when disturbed by the Mexican's movement.

He had seen his brother shot down in front of him on the mad rush out of the canyon in the Black Hills. Now he wished that it could have been him that took the slug and not Shelby. He had only known his brother for a few years and in those years had seen him grow from a gangly youth to a capable, though impatient, young man. Then it was all taken away from him in a hail of bullets.

Gottlieb was dead, along with Jesse. No one knew where Reinhold was. It was he who had led his brother and the others into that canyon. They had relied on him for their safety. It was he whose guard was down that deadly afternoon. He could not forgive himself.

After barely escaping from the canyon with their lives, Stuart and Sanchez holed up for several days in an abandoned mine. Stuart had been slightly wounded in his left arm and was hurt from the fall from his horse. His leg had grown numb with pain and then stiffened until he could no longer walk on it. He writhed in pain for a night and a day, wringing wet with fever. Sanchez kept a fire going and covered his boss with his poncho and a horse blanket until the fever broke and he was able to take water.

When Stuart was able to move around physically, he also started to ruminate mentally on what had happened. He had had no foreboding at all of what was to occur on that deadly afternoon. He felt that he should have sensed that danger was coming. Perhaps the pickings in the Hills had been too easy, and he had lost that sixth sense. They had been so close to avoiding the disaster; in a few days they would have ridden out of the Hills for good.

After a few days rest he traveled into Deadwood, trying to cipher who it was that destroyed his gang. He left Sanchez behind so as not to draw attention. He knew it wouldn't be hard to get information if a person was willing to settle in for a few days and buy a few drinks. After sitting in on a card game with Catlin and a few Deadwood loafers he heard all he wanted. The man who was responsible for his brother's death was a certain Sam Kerlan, and this Kerlan had headed east over the reservation. All that lay out that way was the Missouri River and Ft. Pierre. He wouldn't be too hard to track.

Shortly after, Stuart stumbled upon the resting place of his brother and the others. They were buried in a little patch on Mount Moriah set aside for bandits, whores, drunks, horse thieves, Chinamen and county wards. It was a bleak little tuft of earth where no marker indicated the spot of his brother's eternal rest. Three fresh graves had been dug and he knew one of them contained the earthly remains of Shelby.

At first he planned to shoot down Catlin for his part in his gang's demise but then thought better of it. He did not want to draw unnecessary attention to himself, and he did not want anything to interfere with his vengeance on Sam Kerlan. He would pass through Deadwood another day to take revenge on Catlin and Hiram Drummond.

On his return to his hideout with Sanchez, he made his way back to the canyon of death to claim the gold and money that was buried near the cabin. He stood near the spot where Shelby and Jesse met their maker, rehashing in his mind what he could have done differently to prevent such an outcome.

The night was cold, and he sat before the fire trying to keep warm. He had decided to vacate the comforts of the hotel in Ft. Pierre so as to leave as little a trace of his movements as possible. He'd spoken to the lady in the dry goods store and it wasn't hard to learn as to the whereabouts of Kerlan. The Talbert place down on the Bad River, the lady had informed him, had a visitor from out West. He and Sanchez would pay the place a visit and see for themselves if Kerlan was there.

The Mexican mumbled something in Spanish in his sleep. Stuart threw a limb on the fire and pulled his blanket around him. It would be a long, cold night, warmed only by a dwindling fire and the hate and desire for vengeance that filled Stuart's soul.

***

Benjy loped his pony across an open expanse of prairie, feeling the cool wind against his face. Roy McCrea had sent him out to the west pasture to check for strays, and Benjy went happily about his appointed task. They had been fixing fence near the ranch buildings. Roy knew well that it was not Benjy's favorite pastime. So he sent the boy out, sensing that the youngster was worried about his Pa and uncle and thinking that the trip might get his mind off his concerns.

Benjy rode around the main herd, not wanting to bother the grazing animals. The cattle looked content. The winter had been fairly open, and the herd was still able to forage off prairie grass. Cows weren't like horses, which would dig under a snow cover to find feed. If the feed wasn't under a cow's nose, it would bellow till it starved to death.

He noticed a few steers a half mile or so from the herd and loped over and came along them, moving them back toward the herd. They went along peacefully enough, though lowing softly in complaint.

After moving the steers back into the main herd, Benjy put one leg over the saddle horn and sat comfortably watching the cattle. He was as proud as his father of the herd they had built up over the years. It was a hard life working a cattle ranch on the stark Dakota prairie, but it was the only life Benjy ever knew. There were early mornings when he wished he could sleep just another hour, and long days in the saddle when he would have preferred a rocking chair, but moments like this made it worth all the hardship. One lesson the boy had learned from his father was that patience and hard work over a period of time gathered rewards. Not just material rewards, but also the wealth of knowing that they were building a secure and peaceful life. He was his father's son, and shared his father's understanding of what was good in life.

Benjy's cow pony was growing impatient with its master's musings and moved about anxiously. He put his leg down and found the stirrup with his foot.

"Alright, boy, let's ride around this bunch and head for home."

The cattle were stretched out thinly for the better part of a mile and Benjy cantered the perimeter, far enough from them so as not to disturb their feeding, but close enough to discourage the more adventuresome cows from wandering.

After completing his circuit, Benjy rode back to the Bad and followed it toward the ranch. He stopped for a time at Dead Horse, a small rise along the river, named by Benjy and his brother, where an Indian pony had lain down to die. The years had worn away the pony's flesh and the sun had bleached its bones pearl white. The intact skeleton could still be seen embedded in the hill.

He let his pony take a drink at the river as he looked at the remains of the horse in the hill's side. It was stretched out in such a way as to make it look as though it was at a full run.

Benjy pulled up the reins and moved down the river. He thought of his father and uncle, hoping that they would be home soon. Suddenly, he decided he should stop fooling around, and putting his pony into a lope, he headed for home.

Chapter Twenty-Eight

Stuart and Sanchez had covered that same ground earlier in the day. Stuart had noticed the skeleton of the dead horse, but did not comment to Sanchez. He and Sanchez had little in common, and if times had been different, Stuart would never have associated with him. If it had not been for the war and its terrible aftermath, Stuart likely would have been a tobacco and cotton trader like his father. The forties and fifties had been prosperous times for the Stuarts, and old man Stuart had built up a prosperous business. Gil, as the oldest son, was poised to take over and continue his father's legacy but war came, and young men in gray turned to battle, motivated by dreams of glory and of their love of the old South. The Stuarts had never owned slaves, so Gil felt he was fighting for home and hearth, and an independent way of life, independence as strong and determined as the Southern heart and soul.

He rode now with a Mexican so cruel that even Stuart, hardened by war and loss, was shocked at times. If he tolerated the Mexican at all, it was because of Sanchez's cunning in a fight and of his ability to kill without a second thought.

Yet he could hardly criticize the cruelties of other men, for on many occasions Stuart himself had killed in cold blood. But he rationalized his own actions, convincing himself that he only killed with good reason. He never killed just to see someone die; he did so to cover his trail or to make sure that no living witness could testify to his deeds. When he killed, he felt he killed cleanly and did not allow the victim to suffer for long. This is what separated him from the Mexican; Sanchez clearly took a certain pleasure from seeing someone die.

Stuart's musings now brought him to the task at hand. His brother and the other members of his gang were dead, and so there was no question or doubt about what he had to do. The Mexican understood also, and did not question his boss about where they were going or what they would do. Stuart would kill whoever was responsible for the death of his brother. It was as simple as that. If anyone got in the way; he too would die.

They came to a point on the Bad River where the terrain widened out into a large valley and they could see ranch buildings in the distance. Stuart motioned to Sanchez, and the two riders moved away from the river and up into the small hills above the buildings. There they dismounted their horses and looked down on the Talbert ranch. They could see little activity in and around the place. A man was working fences near the corral buildings. Two small children played in the ranch yard, and a woman was hanging laundry at the back of the house. There was no sign of other men about the place, but Stuart decided to watch awhile to make sure. So far it looked like easy pickings, but he didn't want to ride into any surprises.

Sanchez held the horses below the crest of the hill so as not to create a silhouette on the horizon. Stuart, hunched down, continued to watch the activity at the ranch. Finally, he was convinced no one else was around.

Stuart signaled Sanchez to bring up the horses. As the two mounted, Stuart noticed a certain look on the face of Sanchez. It was a look Stuart had seen before, an excitement in the eyes, a sweating about the beard, a look that reminded him of a mad dog frothing up for the kill.

Chapter Twenty-Nine

Roy McCrea was concentrating on getting a corner post buried deep enough to hold against the rigors of weather and animals, and so did not notice the two riders approaching him. Stuart and Sanchez had their guns drawn, removing any possibility for argument. Roy led them to the house.

Irma was sweeping off the front porch when she looked up to see Roy on foot with two mounted, armed men in back of him.

"What's this?" she questioned no one in particular.

"Irma," Roy answered, "these men here say they're looking for a man named Sam Kerlan. I told them we never heard the name."

Irma sized up the situation. These men were obviously not friends of Sam and wished him harm. Following Roy's lead, she began to nod in the affirmative when little Laura chirped up.

"You mean Uncle Sam?"

"Yes," Stuart responded to the little girl. "We're old friends of your Uncle Sam and are looking forward to seeing him."

As he waved his pistol, Sanchez dismounted and went into the house, emerging quickly with little Sammy by the scruff of the neck.

"No one here 'cept this little Nino," he said with a sneer.

Stuart dismounted and walked up on the porch, taking in the environs of the ranch yard as he did so.

He again addressed the little girl, letting Irma and Roy know by the wave of his hand that he would tolerate no interference.

"Darling, where is your Uncle Sam?"

Laura thought for a second before innocently answering, "He and Daddy are out after rustlers."

Stuart gently patted the little girl on the head.

"I'll ask this just once," he said sternly to Irma and Roy. "When are they expected back?"

Roy shuffled his feet in the dirt for a moment or so. He knew it was his responsibility to safeguard Irma and the children. Not being straightforward with men like this could mean sudden death for his charges.

"They've been gone three days. They're expected back any time now," he answered flatly.

"Now that was easy and I might add, smart. We don't want to hurt you folks and if you do as we say no one will be harmed."

Somehow these words didn't comfort Roy. Both he and Irma knew they were still in grave danger.

Stuart directed everyone into the house and had them sit together at the kitchen table. He instructed Sanchez to keep a watch outside and told Irma to prepare a meal. Stuart kept watch in a large chair, removed from the rest, with a Winchester rifle across his lap. Irma nervously went about preparing a noon meal.

After a time Roy broke the heavy silence.

"What do you want with Sam?"

"Let's just say I owe him something and I've come to make payment," Stuart drawled.

The answer had an unsettling affect on Roy. He knew Sam's life was in danger. He knew, too, that everyone was at risk, and that it was up to him to do something. But timing was everything; one false move could mean instant death.

Irma finished cooking the meal, and Stuart directed her to take a plate of food out to Sanchez. The Mexican grabbed the plate that Irma handed him and began to devour the food.

"Oh, by the way," Stuart said to Roy as he calmly ate his meal. "You try something and I'll kill not only you, but the woman and the children. You don't know who you're dealing with here. Don't try to be a hero."

Roy swallowed hard and stared with a growing hatred at the unwelcome and threatening guest.

***

Benjy watched the activity at the ranch with growing concern. He had stopped on a little rise above the ranch just as Roy was leading two armed men up to the house. He observed keenly as the men talked with his mother and Roy on the porch and then watched as everyone went into the house except the large man, who sat himself down in his father's rocker.

Soon his mother came out on the porch and handed a plate of food to the heavy, dark man who took it from her brusquely. Immediately his mother returned to the house.

Benjy sat on his cow pony and watched and worried for some time. He fretted as to what he should do. If he went down to the ranch house he would be just another captive. He did not have any firearms with him, and even if he did, he had the sense to know that a fifteen year old boy would be no match for these strangers. His father and uncle were God knows where and he had little chance of finding them by heading out across the prairie.

He wished his father were here, but he especially wished his Uncle Sam were with him. Though he had known his uncle only a short time, he sensed that Uncle Sam would know what to do in such a situation. Benjy had every confidence in the abilities of his father, but his father was no gunman.

The boy grew more nervous with each passing minute. He felt precious time slipping away, as if an hourglass full of the sands of his mother's and siblings', and Roy's, lives were running out quickly.

Then his mind was made up. He determined that Ft. Pierre would be his best chance of getting immediate help. He turned his pony down the rise and the little horse leaped into a lope. As it hit the open prairie at a full run, it strained every ounce of sinew and muscle at its master's behest.

***

Ben and Sam loped languidly out of Ft. Pierre, thoroughly enjoying the crisp day. Sam was beginning to see the benefits of his brother's way of life, and found himself contemplating life as a rancher with some pleasure. A life full of daily routines and future plans contrasted well with his current lifestyle in which every day might be his last.

The thoughts of his brother were similar. Ben pondered as to how he would get his brother to stay and make his life with them on the Dakota prairie. He felt his brother was searching for something, some new way of life that would allow him to leave behind the harsh realities and cruel demands of a gunman's existence.

Both trails of thought were suddenly interrupted when they noticed Benjy hanging low in his saddle and driving his little cow pony down the river trail as if Satan himself were on his heels.

Sam and Ben moved their horses to opposite sides of the river road, for they saw that Benjy was riding too fast to avoid crashing into them.

Benjy shot between the two riders, pulling up in his saddle when he recognized the blurs as his father and uncle. He pushed forward in his stirrups, leaning back against the cantle and pulling hard on the reins. The little horse almost sat down on its haunches as it came to a skidding stop on the trail. Benjy then pulled the left rein hard, turning the pony in the spot where it stood. The little horse sprang into a short run to where Benjy's father and uncle were watching in amazement.

Benjy was breathing so hard that he couldn't get a word out.

"Take it easy, Son," Ben said to him. "Get your breath before you try to talk."

Benjy nodded vigorously and tried to control his breathing. His uncle moved his horse up beside him and patted the boy on the back until Benjy could get his wind.

"Men," he finally said, "two men have taken Ma, Roy and the kids' captive."

"What men?" Ben shouted.

"Two men in long, white dusters. One of them is fat and wears a sombrero."

Sam winced as if someone had driven a knife into the small of his back. He had brought his wretched, dangerous life to his brother's doorstep.

"They're after me," Sam said in disgust. "The man in the sombrero is a Mexican, Sanchez. The other is Gil Stuart. They're both dangerous snakes."

Ben listened and then said, "O.K., Benjy, you go into Ft. Pierre and wait at the Haggertys until someone comes for you. Sam, you and I will head for the ranch and see what these two men want."

"I know what they want," Sam said as Benjy rode away toward Ft. Pierre. "They want me dead. I'm afraid, Ben, that I put your whole family in danger. I had no idea this would happen or I'd never have come out here."

"We can't think of such things, Sam," Ben answered. "Let's just get to the ranch."

With those words both men spurred their horses and rode in a fury down the river trail.

Chapter Thirty

Gil Stuart had Sanchez spell him for a time in the house as he walked around the out buildings of the ranch. "A substantial place," he thought to himself. He saw that Kerlan's brother knew what he was after in life and had built for himself a place in the sun. He would have done much the same if things had been different, although not on the plains of Dakota. His world would have been of cotton and tobacco, not of cattle. Otherwise, it would have been much the same. He would have married and brought children into the world. The bounty of the Southern way of life would have enveloped them in its warm days and soft nights and their lives would have been gentle, civil and honorable. Gil Stuart kept this wispy dream, a fantasy that helped him escape the harsh realities of a life he felt forced upon him.

He leaned against the corral gate, watching a herd of horses move uneasily against the opposite fence. They knew they had a stranger in their midst.

Gil Stuart thought of his brother and of the other members of his gang who were stone cold dead and buried on the windswept hill above Deadwood. Shelby and Jesse had their young lives taken from them in a blast of gunfire they probably had not even heard.

He remembered a time in the war when his small cavalry outfit was camped near Fredericksburg before the battle of Chancellorsville. Some soldiers were bringing back the dead from skirmish lines set up days earlier. The bodies were laid on the opposite side of the road from their small encampment. After supper, he and his first sergeant had taken a walk passing the dead laid out side by side. Though long used to the sight of dead bodies, this time Stuart was struck by the body of a young Confederate soldier. The soldier was all but a child, with fair skin and long, wheat colored hair. He looked as if he were sleeping; waiting for the nightmare of the war to pass so he might get on with the pleasures of boyhood. The sight disturbed Stuart, but he was only the first of many dead boys he would see, dressed in both blue and gray.

Had evil chosen him or had he chosen evil? If things had been different, would he now be living an honest and upstanding life? Or had the reptile of cruelty slithered into his cradle and wrapped him as a suckling in its glistening length?

Stuart shook off these plaguing doubts. He had long ago cast his lot. There was no turning back, and no forgiveness for the sins he had committed.

***

The two riders squinted against the bright midday sun, taking in the ranch buildings below them.

Ben shifted nervously in his saddle, wondering what to do or to say. Sam, on the other hand, sat stoically, knowing that no matter how all of this turned out, someone was about to die. The thought of his brother's family paying the price for his wayward past stabbed at his heart.

"What do we do?" Ben asked helplessly.

Sam did not speak right away, but only stared at the deceptively peaceful ranch below.

"We just go straight in. It's the only way. If they fight we have to move and move fast. If they talk, we'll talk. They're holding all the cards, Ben, and it's the only way."

Without another word, the two men urged their horses down the hill toward the showdown; their only hope was that no loved ones would die.

Sanchez spotted the two riders coming slowly toward them and yelled to Stuart inside the house. Stuart stepped out onto the porch and watched as the two men drew closer. Stuart told Sanchez to stand in the doorway and keep an eye on the prisoners.

At a distance just within rifle shot, Ben and Sam stopped their horses. Sam raised his arm, more in acknowledgement than in greeting.

Stuart returned the gesture and an uneasy silence settled over the men.

Ben, no longer able to stand the stifling suspense and fear, yelled out to Stuart, "What is it you want?"

Stuart walked down from the porch to the ground in front of the house.

"Well," Stuart said in a barely audible voice, "to start with we'd like your money. Along with that, we'd like your brother there."

Ben turned to Sam who was silently observing the situation.

"I'm sorry about all this, Ben," said Sam, struggling with his emotions, but keeping a cool head and looking for any opportunity.

Sam turned back toward Stuart and cleared his throat.

"Stuart," he shouted in a steady voice, "we can make a deal here. We'll give you all the money we have, and I'll go with you. The family must be left alone."

"Sounds good to me," Stuart responded, "but how do we make the trade?"

Sam knew this part would be difficult and did some quick considering.

"First," he answered Stuart, "you have the family come outside. The wife will give you the money in the house. The family will come out toward us as I come in toward you. I'll give my arms to the hired man as we pass and come in with my money."

Stuart thought for a moment and answered quickly, "All right."

Sanchez brought Irma out onto the porch, and Stuart pointed to her husband and brother-in-law.

"Irma," Ben shouted, "get the money out of the box and give it to these men. Do it now!"

Irma immediately went into the house with Sanchez, and in a short time Sanchez returned with a large box full of paper money.

"Ben," Sam said as this was going on, "when the trade is made, have your guns ready. Have Irma and the kids hunkered down, and you and Roy get your rifles ready to fire. If they shoot at you or charge, return fire. If they don't, leave it alone. They're dangerous men and not to be trifled with. If they kill me right away ignore it unless they come after you."

"But . . . but," Ben stammered.

"If you want your family safe you must do this," Sam continued firmly. "It could be the difference between life and death for them."

Ben could not respond, but by his silence acquiesced to his brother's demands.

Stuart directed Roy, Irma and the children to begin their walk to Ben and Sam. Sam immediately left his brother and rode slowly toward them. At the halfway point he removed his gun belt and his

Henry from its scabbard and handed them to Roy. He smiled wanly at Irma and the children, and Irma said softly through her tears, "Oh, Sam."

At almost the same time Irma, Roy and the children reached Ben, Sam rode up to Stuart and Sanchez.

"Well, Mr. Kerlan," Stuart said in a cynical drawl, "very pleased you could join us. Let's see that money you were talking about."

Kerlan handed Stuart a large black wallet, and Stuart opened it and looked inside.

"My brother's blood money," he said in a low and menacing voice.

Ben huddled Irma and the children behind Cyclone, and he and Roy watched the ranch house. His brother and the other men stood outside for what seemed to Ben a long time. Finally, the heavy man went around to the barn, bringing up the horses, and they mounted up. With Sam in the lead, the three riders started away from the ranch buildings.

At first Ben could not make out which way the riders were heading, but then it became apparent to him they were riding toward the old Indian trail along the Bad River heading southwest.

Ben and Roy watched the riders for some time before taking Irma and the children back to the ranch house. He told Roy to saddle his horse.

Ben went quickly into the house and took two Winchester rifles down from their pegs above the fireplace. He reached into a drawer, withdrew a large box of cartridges, and quickly loaded the rifles.

Irma watched her husband with fear and trepidation. She knew the other two men were gunmen who could easily out master her husband and Roy's abilities. The only one she felt could match such men was Sam, and he was unarmed and would be of little help.

"Ben," she said in as even a voice as she could muster. "Those men are killers and you and Roy can't stand up to them alone. Ride to Ft. Pierre and gather some men to help you."

"There isn't time. Those two will kill Sam as soon as they get out on the trail. We've got to get to them as soon as possible."

At that moment Roy came into the house.

"Horses ready, Ben," he said firmly.

Ben handed Roy one of the Winchesters and the two men left the house without another word.

They mounted, put spurs to flesh, and disappeared from the yard so quickly that they were gone before Irma could come out on the porch.

From the direction they were heading, Roy knew well Ben's intentions. They were going to ride hard, circle the Indian trail, and sit in ambush further up the trail. Ben's knowledge of the area was their only advantage against Sam's captors.

Chapter Thirty-One

The three men rode in silence until they reached the trail along the river.

"Sanchez," Stuart said in a low voice, "you ride ahead and make sure we're not riding into anything. If his brother is anything like Kerlan here, he's bound to make trouble for us."

Sanchez rode off at a trot and disappeared around a bend in the river trail.

"I don't think you have anything to worry about. I told my brother not to force your hand. He's got a family to think about."

"Yea," answered Stuart, "well, I once had a family to worry about but the war took that from me. Men like you and me should only have to worry about ourselves."

"If it's any worth to you, I regret killing those two boys in the hills."

"Well, it's no use to me now, and one of those boys was my little brother. He was the last of my blood, and it was my responsibility to protect him and guide him along."

"Perhaps you should have guided him to a different profession than horse stealing."

"I don't feel that's any much of your business,' Stuart responded curtly. "Besides, there wasn't anything else for me after the war. War has more victims than those who lose their lives."

The two men rode on in silence for some time. A north wind was blowing and there was heaviness in the air that felt like the approach of a winter storm.

"What ever happened to Reinhold? Was he killed?" Stuart asked quickly, suddenly thinking of the gentle German.

"He was wounded in the side. Flesh wound. I let him go," answered Kerlan.

"Well, you're just judge, jury and executioner all rolled up into one, aren't ya?" said Stuart sarcastically. "Now you're going to find out how it feels when other men decide your fate."

"Why don't you just get it over with? Where are you taking me anyway?" Kerlan asked, showing no further remorse.

"I'm going to take you back to Deadwood where you're going to meet your maker with your old friends. I found out from that halfwit companion of yours who paid for the deaths of my brother and men. I just feel it's appropriate that you all die together before the grave of my brother. That way they won't have to carry you up Mount Moriah to bury you," Stuart said, grinning contemptuously.

Stuart again returned to his stony silence. Kerlan rode ahead of him, staring at the trail that would lead him to his death.

Ben and Roy rode hard up and down gullies, through washes and around trees, their horses seemingly in tandem and their bodies leaning hard into their saddles. Away from the river, they hit a flat plain and crossed it at full gallop. Down again into the gullies and hills they rode until they reached the place where Ben felt would be their only opportunity to save his brother's life.

They dismounted the horses and Roy led them down away from the river. Ben climbed a small rise and positioned himself above the river with a good view down the river trail.

After tying off the horses, Roy joined him on the rise. They sat poised and quiet and waited for whoever would ride into their hastily laid trap.

***

Sanchez cantered a few miles' distance from his boss and their captive and settled to an easy walk along the river's path. The path was one the Sioux had used to travel between the Missouri and the Black Hills. But even if he had known it, this history meant nothing to Sanchez.

He was wearying of this land that was turning colder by the day. He longed for the south, for Mexico, but would easily settle for Arizona or New Mexico Territory. He wanted to see some of his own people, to speak Spanish again, and would sell his soul for some tequila and a night or two with a pretty Mexican whore. It was his hope that having captured Kerlan, his boss's business in this country would end and they would soon head south. He had always felt that this land was bad luck, and the shootout in the little canyon in the hills had proven him right.

Sanchez thought of his youth in Mexico. Orphaned young, he had traveled with a band of caballeros, and did their bidding. He blackened boots and fixed tack until, in time; he came of age and joined them in their forays across the Rio Grande. He'd been a thief and a killer most of his life and thought nothing of the difference. But he, like his boss, now felt time catching up with him. The good hideouts were gone. More civilization brought opportunity, but it also brought more law, and with that law gunmen who were at least as good as he was. He did not know what fate held for him and did not often think about it. All he knew was that he wanted to lay low for a while, go someplace warm, drink tequila and lay with a two dollar whore.

Sanchez's wandering thoughts had distracted him from his task. He suddenly heard the rustle of bushes above the rocks, and in the split second it took to turn his eyes to those bushes, a blast reached his ears, and in another instant, his chest seemed to explode under his beard. Sanchez knew no more, thought no more and felt no more. He did not even feel the impact of his huge body as he fell from his horse to the frozen ground.

The rifle's report rang loud along the river road and took Kerlan and Stuart by surprise. In an instant, Kerlan spurred his horse and rode as quickly as he could away from Stuart. Stuart gained his composure, drew his pistol from its holster across his waist and fired at the fleeing Kerlan.

Sam felt the bullet slam into his upper shoulder and felt the rush of blood down his back and side. He crumpled forward in the saddle and rode until he was alongside a deep gully which led down to the river. He jumped off the back of his horse and rolled down the hill, wincing in pain each time his wounded shoulder hit the ground. He felt himself roll into the water and the cold wetness jolted him back from the edge of unconsciousness. He stumbled up stream and looked everywhere for some means of escape, for he knew well that Stuart would soon be upon him.

Looking up the stream, he saw a huge cottonwood whose branches stretched over the water like the cross from the cathedral in Santa Fe. This tree would be Kerlan's only chance for salvation.

Stuart rode his horse up to where Kerlan's gelding stood on the road above the river. He urged his horse slowly down the deep gully as he leaned back deep into his saddle. Reaching the water, he looked up and down the stream. He went downstream for a short time and saw it opened up into a large meadow. He searched the periphery of the bank and saw no sign of Kerlan.

He turned his horse upstream and rode, watching the shoreline as he went.

Kerlan secured himself on the huge cottonwood branch that reached over the water. He hid himself as well as he could, knowing that a sharp eye could spot him resting on the limb.

He reached down into his boot and pulled out a small, two-shot Derringer. He had won the pistol in a card game in Creed, Colorado and many times since had thought about discarding it. Now he held the gun to his chest, knowing this little gun would be his only hope against Stuart's vengeance.

Moving his horse slowly up the stream, Stuart kept a close and vigilant eye on the banks of the river. He looked for anything, a boot mark, a hand mark, any indication of the movement of his prey.

His eyes were fixated on the edge of the water, and this was his final mistake. As he moved under the limb of the cottonwood, he felt a presence and looked up quickly to see Kerlan on the branch above him.

A short report rang out. The small bullet hit Stuart in the face below the left eye, its projection glancing off a facial bone and turning down vertically into his throat. Kerlan could hear Stuart's gurgling curse as he reached for his throat and fell backward into the water.

Kerlan climbed down from the tree and stood by the cottonwood. He leaned against it for a moment and then slowly sat down at its base.

He did not know it, but Stuart, not yet dead, was drowning in the foot deep stream, taking cold water down into his lungs.

Meanwhile, Ben and Roy rode full measure down the river trail, their handguns cocked and ready.

They spotted Sam's gelding munching on grass near the river and pulled their horses up short.

They dismounted and ran along the river trail, looking for any sign of Sam or his captor. Ben's heart was in his throat, he did not know whether he would find his brother dead or mortally wounded.

Roy yelled from down the trail and Ben joined him. They followed a path a horse and rider had made down to the stream. When they reached the water, they looked upstream and down but could see nothing. Roy went downstream and Ben up to try to find some bearings.

In a short time, Ben came upon his brother sitting beside a tree. When he saw him, a sigh of relief exited his chest. He could also see a body floating face down in the cold water.

He walked over and saw that it was Stuart. He put his pistol in its holster, grabbed Stuart's arms, and pulled him to the bank. He walked over to where his brother was sitting against the cottonwood.

"I guess we had a lucky afternoon," he said to him.

"Yea, all told, Lady Luck was with us," Sam returned.

After having spoken, he winced and Ben could see that he was wounded.

Ben looked at his brother's shoulder and could see the exit wound. He leaned his brother forward and could see his blood drenched coat and shirt.

"How bad is it?" he asked, worriedly.

"Passed clean through near as I can tell," Sam answered.

"You're losing a lot of blood," Ben came back. "We've got to get you back to the ranch."

Ben lifted his brother onto Stuart's horse and led it upstream to a place where they could easily climb to the river trail. They met Roy, and Ben instructed him to take the other horses and the bodies back to the ranch.

They climbed the rise and at its summit, Sam started to dismount.

"What are you doing?" Ben asked him in confusion.

"Don't you know its bad luck to ride a dead man's horse?" Sam responded. "I'd just as soon ride my own back."

"I'll go get him for you," Ben offered as he mounted his own horse.

Sam sat down on the trail and watched as Roy led Stuart's horse back down to the river to retrieve its master's body.

Ben brought up Sam's gelding and helped him mount, and the two brothers rode off toward the ranch.

Epilogue

The bodies of Stuart and Sanchez lay in Ben Talbert's barn overnight before the authorities rode over from Ft. Pierre the next morning to gather them up.

An uncommon stillness hung over the ranch. The children were told to be quiet as their mother tended to their uncle's wounds. Ben stayed close to the ranch buildings and let Roy take care of the business off the main place.

Sam was recovering well and took long afternoons out on the porch, smoking cigars and staring off into the snow covered hills. The sun in the afternoons warmed him, and he gained his strength from the sustenance of Irma's fare and the quiet of his mid-day repose.

His brother knew that he was weighing things out, making up his mind. He did not interfere with his musings more than to ask him how he was doing and what he could get for him. Ben hoped that Sam would decide to stay and make his home with them.

One afternoon he rode Cyclone into the yard and found his brother sitting in a rocking chair with a sleeping Laura blanketed in his arms.

He tethered Cyclone to the front post and mounted the steps of the porch.

"Nice afternoon," he said to his brother.

"I was telling little Laura here about our childhood days on the river and it plum tuckered her out," Sam returned.

Irma heard Ben ride up and came out on the porch. She kissed her husband and took her sleeping daughter from Sam and carried her back into the house.

Ben took a chair beside his brother and got out his pipe fixin's and prepared a bowl for himself. He lit the pipe and took several draughts. "You're leaving us, aren't you?" Ben said breathing out a cloud of tobacco smoke.

"They say that nobody knows you like your brother," was all that Sam replied.

"Will you come back someday?" Ben asked.

"Oh, yea, I'll be back."

***

Ben stirred from a hard sleep and sat up in bed. He got out of bed so as not to disturb Irma. He shut the bedroom door behind him and moved through the house and out onto the front porch. It was early and the sun had not yet perched over the horizon.

Ben looked up to the hills around the ranch yard. On the highest hill, the very one he and Benjy had sat upon to look over their holdings, he saw a horseman. It was Sam.

The two brothers watched one another for what seemed the better part of an hour. Finally, Sam raised his hand and Ben returned the gesture.

Sam turned his roan and rode down the leeward side of the hill, his brother watching him as the silent silhouette moved through the mist and out of his field of view.

THE END

S.J. 'Sky' King has worked as a probation officer and horse wrangler, college professor and truck driver. He has taught on the Sioux and Navajo reservations. He travels the west in an ancient Airstream, seeking out new stories from the history, legend and myth of the west.